Praise for
Carlton Mellick III

"Easily the craziest, weirdest, strangest, funniest, most obscene writer in America."
—*GOTHIC MAGAZINE*

"Carlton Mellick III has the craziest book titles... and the kinkiest fans!"
—CHRISTOPHER MOORE, author of *The Stupidest Angel*

"If you haven't read Mellick you're not nearly perverse enough for the twenty first century."
—JACK KETCHUM, author of *The Girl Next Door*

"Carlton Mellick III is one of bizarro fiction's most talented practitioners, a virtuoso of the surreal, science fictional tale."
—CORY DOCTOROW, author of *Little Brother*

"Bizarre, twisted, and emotionally raw—Carlton Mellick's fiction is the literary equivalent of putting your brain in a blender."
—BRIAN KEENE, author of *The Rising*

"Carlton Mellick III exemplifies the intelligence and wit that lurks between its lurid covers. In a genre where crude titles are an art in themselves, Mellick is a true artist."
—*THE GUARDIAN*

"Just as Pop had Andy Warhol and Dada Tristan Tzara, the bizarro movement has its very own P. T. Barnum-type practitioner. He's the mutton-chopped author of such books as *Electric Jesus Corpse* and *The Menstruating Mall*, the illustrator, editor, and instructor of all things bizarro, and his name is Carlton Mellick III."
—*DETAILS MAGAZINE*

Also by Carlton Mellick III

Satan Burger
Electric Jesus Corpse
Sunset With a Beard (stories)
Razor Wire Pubic Hair
Teeth and Tongue Landscape
The Steel Breakfast Era
The Baby Jesus Butt Plug
Fishy-fleshed
The Menstruating Mall
Ocean of Lard (with Kevin L. Donihe)
Punk Land
Sex and Death in Television Town
Sea of the Patchwork Cats
The Haunted Vagina
Cancer-cute (Avant Punk Army Exclusive)
War Slut
Sausagey Santa
Ugly Heaven
Adolf in Wonderland
Ultra Fuckers
Cybernetrix
The Egg Man
Apeshit
The Faggiest Vampire
The Cannibals of Candyland
Warrior Wolf Women of the Wasteland
The Kobold Wizard's Dildo of Enlightenment +2
Zombies and Shit
Crab Town
The Morbidly Obese Ninja
Barbarian Beast Bitches of the Badlands
Fantastic Orgy (stories)
I Knocked Up Satan's Daughter
Armadillo Fists
The Handsome Squirm
Tumor Fruit
Kill Ball
Cuddly Holocaust
Hammer Wives (stories)
Village of the Mermaids
Quicksand House

CYBERNETRIX

CARLTON MELLICK III

ERASERHEAD PRESS
PORTLAND, OREGON

ERASERHEAD PRESS
205 NE BRYANT
PORTLAND, OR 97211

WWW.ERASERHEADPRESS.COM

ISBN: 1-62105-076-9

Printed in the USA.

AUTHOR'S NOTE

When I came up with the idea for my book *Haunted Vagina* I thought it was perhaps the stupidest idea on the face of the planet. So, of course, I *had* to write it. I thought it would be even funnier to approach the story as if it were conventional mainstream fiction. Writing such a ridiculous story in a straight, serious manner was completely hilarious to me. So that's what I did. But I don't think anybody (aside from myself) got the joke. That's okay, though, because I'm used to being the only person who laughs at my jokes.

When I came up with the idea for *Cybernetrix* I realized it was an even stupider idea than Haunted Vagina. So, of course, I *had* to write it. And I wrote it in an even more serious, straightforward manner than Haunted Vagina. I put all of my heart and soul into writing it. It's the least bizarro of any of my books, yet it is also probably the weirdest thing I will ever write. Not because the story is weird, but because the fact that I wrote it at all is weird, and the fact that some people say it's the best book I've ever written is weird. I personally wouldn't say it's my best book, but if you're a fan of the movie *Tron* you'll probably like it.

By the way, if you haven't seen the movie Tron you better watch that before you read this book. In fact, you should watch Tron before reading this book even if you have seen it before. Cybernetrix is pretty much a Tron parody, so there's really no point in reading this book without having seen it. Besides, it's one of the best movies ever made.

These days, I'll only write a book in one long writing session. I check into a hotel room and shut myself off from the world. I write the book from beginning to end over the course of several days in that little room. I don't check out until the book is done.

I wrote this book at the Sylvia Beach Hotel on the Oregon Coast during a novel-writing marathon with fellow writer

Daniel Scott Buck. The Sylvia Beach Hotel is an interesting place. It is a hotel designed for readers and writers to have a quiet relaxing getaway. Each room of the hotel is named after a different author and decorated accordingly. I stayed in the JRR Tolkien room, which had maps of Middle-earth on the wall, a replica of Bilbo's sword *Sting*, a toadstool lamp, a handcrafted wooden hobbit bed, and live vines growing down from the bed frame. It was pretty cool and actually pretty affordable. Daniel was next door in the Robert Louis Stevenson room writing his children's book *Marvin the Mosquito*.

It was the first time I stayed at the Sylvia Beach Hotel. Normally I stay in cheap motels that smell of cricket skin and wet dog. This was much different. I spent most of my time writing on a wicker chair, sleeping only a couple hours at a time, and brainstorming future chapters while walking on the beach. In the evenings, everyone in the hotel ate dinner together at the same table in the basement. We had crab cakes and creamed sea scallops. We drank wine and discussed literature, politics, and history. Then Daniel and I went upstairs to the study. We drank hot spiced wine and discussed ways to improve the Portland literary community.

It was the kind of setting that would have been inspirational to someone writing classy, artsy poetry or *fine* literature. However, I was writing Cybernetrix. We're talking about a book where a Tron-like guy ejaculates blue laser-sperm onto glowing Tron girl breasts. Yeah, it's some classy stuff. And I wrote it at the Sylvia Beech Hotel. It made me feel really awkward at dinner when people would ask me: "So what are you writing about?" And I would have to say: "Tron people... having sex." Then I would get a snooty you-don't-belong-here look.

But that's the kind of writer I am. I write about haunted vaginas and Tron sex. If that's not *literary* enough for you, then too bad. Art has nothing to do with good taste.

CHAPTER ONE
NEO TOKYO CRIMEWAVE

🛸 👾 🛸

Wesley Allen Scott's first day at his new job was to begin in exactly twenty-three minutes, but he had yet to get out of bed. He was busy staring at the glow-in-the-dark Devo poster on his ceiling and debating whether or not to call in sick. He wondered if they would fire him if he didn't show up for his first day. He wondered if he cared. It had taken him twelve weeks to actually find a company willing to hire him and he loathed the idea of going through the job-hunting process again. He'd rather get shot in the face. If he did decide to go to work that day, he hoped somebody would shoot him in the face before he got there.

Wesley was depressed. He never used to be such a depressing character. He used to be the happiest and most optimistic person among his group of friends. He used to think he could conquer the world. When he was a teenager, he was the most creative and gifted student in his entire school. A brilliant storyteller and an exceptional artist; all of his teachers told him so. With his talent, Wesley planned to work in the comic book industry. He wanted to create something like Neil Gaiman's *The Sandman*. He wanted to be famous.

But his dreams were slowly crushed over time—a common fate for dreams. He'd lost all confidence in his ability and he began to believe that there was no hope for anyone to succeed in the creative world anymore. He thought that it was impossible. He thought that luck and connections were the only way to succeed, and talent accounted for nothing.

11

That day, he had finally given up on his dreams and was about to face reality.

That day, he had to go to work.

Wesley pulled himself out of bed and folded himself into the shower. He was so nervous about facing his first day in the real world that he drank three 40s of King Cobra last night. His head felt like it was bruised and filled with sand as the hot water poured over his brand new Supercuts hairstyle.

He knew he should hurry, but his body wouldn't let him move any faster than zombie-speed. He'd show up for work that day, even if he was late, because he had nowhere else to go. If they fired him for not showing up on time it would probably make his day. But he knew his money was running out fast. He needed a pay check and he needed it last week. He wished his parents were still alive so they could bail him out of this situation.

Wesley's parents adopted him when they were in their fifties. They were rather wealthy and spoiled him with M.A.S.K. action figures and Andre the Giant themed birthday parties. He'd never worked a day in his life, because he never needed to. The Scotts were approaching their seventies by the time Wesley went off to college. His mother died in a car accident during his freshman year, while he was taking body shots off of half-naked girls in Mexico for Spring Break. His father died of a stroke midway through his last year of college.

After his father's death, Wesley inherited a large sum of money. It was enough for Wesley to survive off of for quite a long time. Just before exams, he dropped out of college and left his old life behind. He moved to Portland, OR, the birthplace of Dark Horse Comics. He heard that there were many artists and writers who actually made a living off of their art out there, no matter how strange or uncommercial it was, so that's where he decided he wanted to live. He was going to chase his dream, even if he did it without the support of friends or family.

It was the loneliest and most exciting time of his life.

When Wesley got out of the shower, he stood naked in front of an oscillating fan. It was a freezing way to dry off, but it woke him up. He blinked hard like he was trying to remove a pair of contact lenses and looked for a couple of silver shopping bags.

His room was cluttered with comic books, Dungeons and Dragons figurines, Rubik's cubes, jelly babies, Atari 64 games, He-Man coloring books, action figures from the Star Wars: the Next Generation television series (including a rare mint condition Taldo Fett figure), a collection of kung fu dance movies on blu-ray laser disc, and a Hawaiian Punch board game.

He found the shopping bags under a Max Headroom poster and dumped the contents onto his bed. Over the weekend, Wesley had purchased several new business casual outfits at Diamond's in the mall. He hated business casual attire even more than professional attire. There was something about Izod alligator shirts that disturbed him. He frowned at the little embroidered reptile on the left breast of the shirt as he ripped off the tag and slipped it on.

Once he was all dressed and ready to go, the reflection of himself in the mirror made him want to cry. His long hair and soul patch were gone and probably never coming back. All of his tattoos were covered up. His lip and eyebrow piercings had already sealed up. He looked like a completely different person than he had been earlier that year. He didn't like this unfamiliar person in the mirror at all. There was a bit of himself that he recognized, but for the most part he had become a hollowed and tainted version of his former self.

👾 👾 👾

Wesley didn't get shot in the face as he took the bus to the Ban roll-on building in downtown Portland. It's called the Ban roll-on building by the locals because the dome on the top of the building made it look like a tube of Ban deodorant. He decided to go around the corner for a can of Tab and a sausage McMuffin instead of entering. He went down to Pioneer Square and watched the break-dancers for a while, then gave some change to a pseudo homeless guy carrying an ipod ghetto blaster on his shoulder. The boombox was playing the 12th or maybe 13th release of The Fat Boys. Wesley wasn't one to keep up with popular music, but he recognized the Fat Boys. They had been around since he was a kid. Two of them weren't even really all that fat anymore.

After he ran out of excuses to stay outside, Wesley took the elevator up to the WinCorp office on the fourteenth floor. He wiped away a glob of McMuffin juice that had found its way onto the fly of his pants. The stain left behind looked like he had peed himself a little.

Somehow Wesley was hired by WinCorp, a computer software company, despite being a 27-year-old with absolutely no prior job experience and no college degree. It was all because of sheer luck, Wesley believed. The manager, George Rickman, seemed to be in a really good mood that day. It turned out that Rickman's daughter went to the same out-of-state University as Wesley. For some reason, that was reason enough for Rickman to take a liking to him. Wesley just smiled and laughed at Rickman's jokes. They used up so much time chit-chatting that they didn't spend a whole lot of time going over the resume. Rickman didn't even realize that Wesley never received his college degree, nor did he realize that his previous (and only) employer, Bouncing Lobster Comics, was just Wesley's own self-publishing comic book company that never made a dime.

It seemed to Wesley that it was more important to click personally with a job interviewer than it was to impress with a resume.

14

When Wesley arrived ninety-eight minutes late, Rickman wasn't the jolly balding pal he seemed to be during the job interview. He was busy shouting at somebody through the phone in a thick New Jersey accent. It sounded like it was his wife or daughter.

"Sit," Rickman told Wesley as he entered his office.

Wesley sat down.

"Listen," Rickman told the person on the phone. "Listen to me. Are you listening? Listen up. I want you to go... shut up for a minute. I want you to go to Gillian's and get the DeLorean. Tell her... I don't care. Tell her you're sorry about the pasta salad and the couch. Tell her I'll buy her a new one if she wants, I don't care... It's not going to kill you. Then go to the clinic and see Bobbie. Tell Bobbie you'd rather keep the finger. Don't worry... it happens all the time. You're being paranoid."

Mr. Rickman caught Wesley's eyes and nodded at him.

"Listen to me... Susan?" Rickman continued. "I've got to get going. It'll be fine. Just put pressure on it. It's nothing to cry about. Call me when it's over. Okay?" Then Rickman smiled and laughed into the phone. "Okay. Bye, sweetie. Good luck."

Then he hung up the phone and his faux smile turned into a frown.

He groaned. "Always on a freakin' Monday."

Wesley tried to nod.

"So, three first names guy, right?"

"Huh?" Wesley said.

"Scott Allen something?"

"Wesley Allen Scott."

"Kind of late aren't we, Wesley Allen Scott?" Rickman laughed as if joking, but Wesley could read annoyance behind the laugh.

"Sorry," Wesley said. "I got on the wrong bus."

"Smells like it," Rickman said.

Wesley didn't know what he meant by that.

"You'll need to be clocked in and working before 8:00 everyday. Even one minute late is a point against you. Five points against you within a year and you'll be reprimanded."

"It won't happen again," Wesley said.

"I suggest leaving home half an hour earlier everyday for the next month or two," Rickman said with a faux smile, "Just to be on the safe side."

Wesley lowered his head to a picture of Rickman with that same faux smile on his face. In the picture, Rickman was standing in the woods, wearing a fisherman's vest and holding a large rainbow trout from a line. Wesley wondered if Rickman had been putting on a phony smile at work for so long that he didn't know how to smile for real anymore. Wesley wondered if Rickman used the faux smile in the picture because he knew he would be displaying it in his office. Next to the fishing picture, there were three pictures of Rickman's family. There was a picture of his daughter when she was a little girl and there was a picture of his wife with his daughter when she was a baby and there was a picture of his wife, himself, and his daughter all grown up (a big-haired girl with an awkward smile and a high shiny forehead). Wesley wondered why Rickman's family photos faced outward, where Rickman couldn't see them. It was as if he had the pictures in his office not so he could look at them himself, but because he wanted to show them off to everyone else. Or maybe he just had the photos in his office because not having family photos would have been weird, and so maybe he faced them outward to make sure that nobody thought he was weird.

"You've got training videos to watch today," Rickman said. "I've got meetings most of today so I'll have your in-charge, Chuck, take care of you."

"Sounds good," Wesley said.

Wesley decided that shooting himself in the face after he got home from work sounded even better.

👾 👾 👾

Wesley could tell Chuck Nelson was a dick just by the way he parted his wavy blond hair. He reminded Wesley of Roy Stalin from the movie Better Off Dead, the preppy ski team champion who bullied the underdog/hero Lane Meyer and stole his girlfriend.

Rickman didn't introduce Wesley to Chuck, he just pointed him out across the sea of cubicles and then closed his office door. When Wesley approached the in-charge, Chuck was smiling with large glimmering white teeth at a young brunette with puffy crimped bangs and large pink hoops for earrings. Chuck didn't have a smooth way of flirting, but the young girl, probably too young to buy beer, seemed drawn in by his charms.

Wesley stayed back a couple cubicles, hesitant to interrupt Chuck while he was trying to convince the girl to go out with him. The girl was shy, though, and blushed at the yuppie instead of giving him an answer. Chuck proceeded to explain all of the great things about himself: he plays racket ball every Tuesday and ultimate Frisbee every Sunday, he loves Phil Collins and all of the Phil Collins rip-off bands that have come out in the past few years, he throws Saturday Night Live parties every Saturday Night, he drives one of those new DeLorean Falcons that look kind of like a cross between a DeLorean DMC-12 and a miniature Millennium Falcon on wheels.

After several minutes of watching Chuck raise his eyebrows and bounce his hair from side to side at Puffy-Haired Girl, Wesley began inching his way toward them. Chuck continued to talk about his car. Wesley wasn't a fan of any new cars. He liked some of the old cars of the 60's and 70's but ever since DeLorean became the top car manufacturer in the country three decades ago, almost every car you see now resembles a spaceship. Almost all of the cars have gull-wing doors that open vertically, rather than horizontally, except for the doors on the Dodge DT that slide open like the side of a minivan even though it is a small two-door sports car.

Wesley didn't say anything, but tried to get Chuck's attention through facial expressions. Chuck made eye contact with him but ignored him. Eventually, the puffy-haired girl pointed Wesley out to the yuppie.

"Can I help you?" Chuck said in an aggravated tone, even though he had a large smile on his face.

"I'm Wesley," Wesley said.

They stared at each other for a minute.

"Well," Chuck said, "good for you."

Chuck looked at Puffy-Haired Girl and burst into an exaggerated laugh. The laugh seemed like it had been practiced in front of a mirror, designed to make him sound manly and charming even when he's being a pompous douche. The girl giggled as well, not because she thought Chuck had said anything funny but because she was nervous.

"It's my first day," Wesley said. "Mr. Rickman told me you would take care of me."

"What do you think I am, your mom?" Chuck said, trying to be funny again but Puffy-Haired Girl didn't laugh.

"Those were his words, not mine."

Chuck cocked his head and made a retarded face at Puffy-Haired Girl, pretending to mimic Wesley's confused, helpless expression. He composed himself after he realized that Puffy-Haired Girl was no longer paying attention to him.

"I'm just joking with you, pal," Chuck said, slapping him hard on the shoulder. "I'll set you up."

Wesley could tell he was just pretending to be friendly and was actually pissed off, as if Chuck blamed him for ruining his chances to score with Puffy-Haired Girl.

👾 👾 👾

Chuck brought Wesley to a small empty cubicle.

"You're right across from me," Chuck said, smiling and

exposing his white teeth.

This close to him, Wesley noticed how horribly fake his tan looked. It looked like he was wearing a thick coat of red and orange makeup.

"Hang ten here for a while," Chuck said. "I'll track down the training videos and get you going on those."

While he was waiting, Wesley reflected on his life and the events that led him to WinCorp.

After he moved to Portland, Wesley was able to survive off of his inheritance for six years. During this time, he worked on a comic called Neo Tokyo Crimewave. It was a postmodern surrealistic cyberpunk story about Yakuza in a futuristic version of Tokyo. Dark Horse Comics wasn't interested in it, though. It was too postmodern, too *weird*. Although Dark Horse had released some unusual comics in its time, they just weren't able to sell anything that experimental. Wesley didn't let this discourage him, though. Even though it was his dream to create something for Dark Horse Comics, he still knew that he had the talent to make it someday.

Wesley woke up every morning at 8:00am, just like he had a regular day job. He worked ten hours a day, sometimes longer, writing and illustrating his series. Eventually he got into indie comics, and realized that a lot of people started independent companies to release their own comic books. That's when Wesley started Bouncing Lobster Comics. He got his comics into a lot of stores around town. He wasn't very good at marketing, but he sold a couple hundred copies of each issue. A lot of the people in the local DIY comic scene thought he was one of the best illustrators in town. He even had a few fans who asked him to sign copies of his books.

But his business sense was poor. He didn't make very much money per copy sold. Not enough to make a living once the inheritance ran out. After a while, the indie comic scene started to die in Portland. The annual comic cons became stagnant and depressing. The other indie comic artists didn't have passion for it anymore. Most of them were even less successful than Wesley. There was a lot of petty in-fighting. One by one, they lost interest in creating comic books and retired their pens in order to watch more television. They didn't meet up on Wednesdays at the Amnesia Brewery anymore. They didn't do much of anything.

But Wesley refused to give up hope. Even when he was the last from his scene, he kept trying to succeed. He worked harder than ever. There was nothing that was going to stand in his way.

Unfortunately, the loss of interest wasn't only in his fellow comic book creators. Readers of comic books seemed to lose interest in comics as well. His comics sold less and less over time. The comic stores stopped carrying his books, most of them couldn't afford to carry many comics anymore. The only comics that were doing any good were the Buffy the Vampire Slayer spin-offs.

Eventually, Wesley decided to throw in the towel as well. He was coming to the end of his six years of inheritance, and knew that he would have to give up on his dream and get a regular job like everyone else. People have always said, "Life sucks, and then you die," but Wesley never wanted to believe that. He wanted to believe that life was what you made it. He wanted to believe that anything was possible. But reality was a bitch that he was only beginning to understand.

👾 👾 👾

After an hour of sitting there, Wesley stood up and peeked out over the sea of cubicles. He saw that Chuck was over by the Puffy-Haired Girl again, and he probably hadn't even begun to search for the training videos yet. Wesley didn't mind, though. He had no problem sitting there, doing nothing.

The room was filled with maybe seventy or eighty cubicles. Many people seemed to be chatting with their cubicle neighbors rather than working. There was a clamor of clacking keyboards and soft voices on telephones, but the office seemed a lot more laid back than Wesley imagined it would be. One of the cubicles was decorated with balloons and confetti, with a large glittery banner that read "Happy Birthday, Jules!" taped to the balloon strings. On the far wall, there was a picture of a large cartoon pizza with arms and legs that had a dialog bubble saying "Red Team Pizza Party: only 340 points to go!" There were similar pizza drawings for a blue team and a yellow team, but they weren't doing as well as the red team. Their pizza drawings also didn't look as happy and colorful as the red team's pizza.

On an adjacent wall, there was a poster handwritten with pink and green highlighters that read "Friday is wacky hat day!"

Then Wesley realized that working in an office was a lot like being in the third grade.

🐛 ⚙ 🐛

As Wesley turned his head to scan the rest of the room, he found that his vision was suddenly blocked by a plump smiling head with a little mustache.

"Howdy neighbor!" said the smiling head.

Wesley jumped back. There was a chubby middle-aged man peeking over his cubicle wall. He had bright red cheeks, tiny glasses, and a combover so thin that Wesley assumed it had to have been done as a joke.

"Don," said the head, all Wesley could see was his head. "Don Conway."

"Wesley Scott," said Wesley.

Don rounded the corner and entered Wesley's cubicle so they could shake hands. He was a short man with a big round belly and a cowboy belt buckle.

"I like your shirt," Don said in an Oklahoma accent.

Wesley looked down and realized he was wearing the exact same alligator shirt as Don. The shirt was much tighter on Don, though, and it showed off his manboobs. Don didn't seem at all ashamed of his belly or manboobs.

"It's like we're twins," Don said, and laughed.

Although it was a lame joke, Don's laugh seemed genuine. He didn't seem to be fake like Chuck or Rickman.

"Yeah," Wesley said.

"You'll be working with me," Don said. "It's just the two of us and Chuck in our department. Chuck used to have your job but he was promoted after Amy left. I still see Amy almost every night though. We play Cybernetrix together."

Wesley realized that this Don guy was kind of weird.

"So what do you like to do," Don asked, "besides dressing up like me?"

Wesley felt awkward telling him. "I write small press comics."

"Have you written any Cybernetrix comics? I always wanted to write a Cybernetrix comic."

"Umm, no," Wesley said. "I created my own series called Neo Tokyo Crimewave." Wesley paused to see if Don might have heard of it before, but the chubby man just smiled and nodded his head "I don't really do anything anymore, though. I've kind of lost interest in creating comic books now that nobody reads them anymore. I've kind of lost interest in life in general."

Wesley didn't know why he just said that. He felt like crying.

"Do you play Cybernetrix?" Don asked, scratching his little mustache.

"What is that?" Wesley asked.

"You've never heard of Cybernetrix? The biggest thing in the history of online gaming?

"I haven't played any video games since the Atari 64."

"Where have you been, buddy? The Atari 64 ain't hip anymore. This is Cybernetrix, dude. Get with the times!"

Wesley wondered why a middle-aged redneck was instructing him on what was hip.

"Haven't you heard about it on the news? In magazines?"

"No. Are the graphics really good or something?"

"Really good? No, they aren't really good. They are out of this world!" Don was getting excited and his voice was becoming really loud. "First of all, it isn't just a video game. It is a world. It is a completely different reality within the game system."

Wesley didn't understand.

"Your consciousness is uploaded into the game console," Don continued. "You actually go inside of the game world. I can't believe you've never heard of this!"

"Are you serious?" Wesley was convinced there was something wrong with Don.

"Yes!" Don cried. "You can't taste or smell anything, but you can see, hear, and feel everything in the Cybernetrix world just the same as you would in reality."

"How does it work?" Wesley asked. "Do you have to wear some kind of full body suit or something?"

"No. Like I said, your mind is actually uploaded over the internet to the game world. They explained it on 20/20 a couple months ago. It has something to do with lucid dreaming. You're actually asleep or half-asleep and the computer controls your dream so that everyone logged on is dreaming the same thing. I don't really know, but it doesn't feel at all like a dream. It feels completely real."

"What's the game about?" Wesley asked.

"It takes place in this glowing neon world," Don said. "Have you ever seen Tron?"

"Yeah."

"Well, the world is like the world in Tron. Actually, it's exactly like the world in Tron. Actually, the game was supposed to be called Tron World, but it's not a child-friendly game so Disney wouldn't let Atari call it that. So they called it Cybernetrix. Have you ever seen the movie Cybernetrix?"

"No."

"Not many people have. It was a B-movie rip-off version of Tron, made around the same time. It was horrible. It was pretty much exactly like Tron but the effects were really substandard. The only reason anyone watched it was for the T and A. The good characters in Cybernetrix were green rather than blue, and the evil characters were purple rather than red. Instead of the Master Control Program, there was the Overlord Program. Instead of the lightcycles, there were lazerbikes. They even spelled laser with a Z. It was a terrible movie. The game is amazing though. Amazing!"

"Don, calm down," Chuck said outside of Wesley's cubicle. "I can hear you yelling all the way across the room."

"Oh, sorry," Don said. "I'm really excited today."

"You need to keep that ADD in check, pal," Chuck said, and made a retarded ADD face at Wesley. Wesley smiled with one side of his mouth because he didn't know what else to do.

"Just kidding," Chuck said. "What are you guys doing, anyway?"

"I was telling him about Cybernetrix," Don said. "Can you believe he's never heard of it before?"

"So?" Chuck said. "Maybe he has a life. Only complete dorks waste their time playing that game."

"If you're calling me a dork I'm allowed to sue," Don said.

"I'm just joking around," Chuck said. "By dorks, I didn't mean you, I meant... other people who waste their lives playing that game."

"It's not a waste of life if you ask me," Don said. "It's more fun than anything I've done in the real world, that's for sure."

"Do you even do anything outside of work besides play that game?" Chuck said.

"Not really," Don said, "besides eating and sleeping and catching the occasional movie. What can I say? I'm obsessed."

"You're beyond obsessed, my friend."

"Have you ever thought about playing?" Don asked.

"I've got better things to do," Chuck said. Then he whispered in Wesley's ear, "Like Shelly over there," as he pointed at Puffy-Haired Girl ten cubicles down.

"You guys don't know what you're missing," Don said, stepping back into his cubicle. "It's like being inside a whole new world. I'm telling you, there's nothing like it."

"Get back to work," Chuck said, rolling his eyes cartoonishly at Wesley.

Chuck was about to wander off when Wesley stopped him.

"You find those training tapes?" Wesley asked.

"I'm on it," Chuck said, tapping his forehead as he back-stepped toward the break room.

👾 👾 👾

Wesley went to Taco De Carlos for lunch and then waited in his cubicle for another hour. Chuck seemed to have gone home for the day.

"Wes," Don said, in a whisper, his head sticking out over the cubicle wall.

"It's Wesley," Wesley said.

"Wesley," he whispered. "Come over here."

Wesley wiped the drool from his shoulder and moved into Don's cubicle. It was strangely warmer in his cubicle, and it was filled with fan art prints of Tron (or more likely Cybernetrix) characters. There were also a few beanie care bears and a picture of Adrian Edmondson, who played the 19th incarnation of The Doctor in the longest running science-fiction television series of all time: Doctor Who.

"Check it out," Don said.

Wesley looked at Don's computer screen. It was the official Cybernetrix website. Don scrolled him through screen shots of the game. It pretty much looked like a bunch of people hanging out in a virtual world similar to that of Tron. There were pictures of lazerbikes on a game grid. There were pictures of green-glowing people throwing electronic Frisbees at purple-glowing people.

"It looks exactly like this when you play," Don said. "Only you're inside of the game."

"It sounds cool," Wesley said. "But I have to admit, I'm finding it all hard to believe. It seems like too huge of a leap in gaming technology to be true."

"Oh, it's leaps and bounds past any of its competitors. It's going to take years before any other game will reach this level of sophistication. At least that is what people say on the Cybernetrix message boards. But it's not the first mind-loader game. About eight years ago they started experimenting with this technology, but the games were very basic. Only one person could play at a time. The graphics were really cheap, a lot like those old Atari 2600 games, and they didn't incorporate the sense of touch very well. You could still feel yourself sitting in your chair at home and the only sensation you'd get is a slight buzzing against your temples when you'd get shot."

Wesley imagined what it would be like to have his brain downloaded into an Atari 2600 game. The thought of blocky 2-bit creatures chasing after him didn't sound fun at all.

"There were only a few games made and they never caught on," Don continued. "In fact, I don't think they ever made it to market. There were some pirated versions that you could buy on the internet, but I didn't hear about them until after Cybernetrix came out and nothing is worth playing anymore now that there's Cybernetrix."

"Well, it sounds pretty cool," Wesley said. "I bet it's expensive though."

"It's worth it," Don said. "Trust me. The hardware is about $100. A subscription is $200 a month or $1500 a year. A free 10 day trial comes with the hardware."

"Seems way too high for a video game," Wesley said.

"But it's not a video game! It's a fantasy world that is as real as this office. Think about it this way: for $100, you can take a 10 day vacation from reality. Imagine if you could teleport from home to Hawaii any time you wanted, for $200 a month!"

"But it's not Hawaii, it's some cheesy Tron rip-off world."

"Yeah, but the 'netrix is even better than Hawaii. You have to play it to see what I mean."

"I guess if you played it all the time I could see the price being worth it," Wesley said, "but if you got bored with video games quickly it would be a waste of money. I don't know, I guess it's probably cool."

"So what do you say?" Don asked.

Wesley looked confused.

"Do you want to play it?" Don asked.

"I don't know."

"Come on," Don said. "Everybody has to play Cybernetrix at least once."

"Well, I'll probably play it some time," Wesley said.

"Tonight?" Don asked.

Wesley shook his head. "Maybe after I get my first paycheck. I'm broke."

"I'm sure you can drum up a measly $100 somewhere," Don said. "Put it on a credit card."

"I don't use credit cards," Wesley said.

Don burst out of his chair and scribbled something on a post-it note. "Here," he said. "If you change your mind, meet us at 7pm on platform 023X. We meet there every night."

Wesley didn't want the sticky note, but it was already stuck to his index finger.

Don raised his mustache at him like he was raising an eyebrow. "I'm telling you, you don't know what you're missing."

Before Wesley knew it, the work day was over. Chuck had never returned with those training videos. His computer was still on, but he must have gone home for the day at lunchtime without telling anyone. Wesley wondered if he went home with Shelly, the girl with the puff-ball bangs. No, he said to himself as he left the building, she's still at her work station. She looked up at Wesley as he left the building and smiled at him. There was something about her smile that made him feel good. It was a genuine smile. Even though her hairstyle was way too trendy for his tastes, she did have a nice face. She was way too good for Chuck Nelson.

🕱 👾 🕱

On his way home, Wesley Allen Scott realized that he was no longer depressed. Perhaps he felt good because he made it through his first day of work okay or maybe because Shelly's smile gave him a good feeling that he was still carrying with him.

Whatever the cause, Wesley was in a good enough mood to stop by the video game store to get the hardware to play Cybernetrix. It wasn't $100 like Don said, it was more like $150, and the trial was a 7-day-trial not a 10-day-trial, but Wesley got it anyway. The box was the size of a stereo system. It had a picture of a green-glowing cyber warrior throwing a power disc at a purple-glowing warrior on an electronic blue grid.

He hoped that it was as fun as Don had told him. He liked the idea of having an escape from reality, and this seemed like a better idea than drinking a bunch of malt liquor as he had originally planned.

CHAPTER TWO
LAZERBIKE FIGHT

When Wesley got home, he heated up a couple of microwave burritos and ate them while watching a little television. Electric Boogaloo 5 was on AMC, but he only caught the end of it. After changing his clothes to sweats and a t-shirt, he opened the Cybernetrix box and tried to figure out how it worked.

Inside, there was a black one-size-fits all flexible plastic helmet. It was three times as heavy as a motorcycle helmet and twice as big. There were also a couple cords, a power strip, and a small control board. The guy at the game store told him that he didn't need an internet connection to play the game, he just needed a cell phone account.

"That's how they get ya," Wesley told himself, realizing that he'd have to not only pay $200 a month to play the game, he'd also have to pay for the cell phone minutes.

There wasn't much of an instruction manual, but there was a warning guide twenty pages long. All Wesley had to do was sign on to the system via the control board and enter a new user name and password. Everything else would be explained to him within the game world.

The control board read: Please secure connection helmet.

Wesley put the helmet on his head and placed the suction-sensors in the correct places on his forehead.

The control board read: Please secure your posture.

Wesley didn't know what it meant by that. He moved on.

The control board read: Please select destination platform.

Wesley looked at the sticky note in his pocket and typed in "023X."

The control board read: Ready to launch? Y/N.

Wesley clicked yes.

🕹 👾 🕹

Wesley felt a whirring vibration within the helmet as it started. His scalp began to tingle. The tingle became a throbbing pulse that stretched from his head down to his toes. His skin became numb. Then he couldn't feel anything. His sense of feeling clicked off like a light switch. He rubbed his hands together, but there was no sensation at all. He could hear and see his hands rubbing together, but he couldn't feel them.

Then Wesley dropped sideways onto the floor. He could hear the thud of his head hitting the carpet, but he didn't feel it. His motor functions had just clicked off like his sense of touch. He should have read the warnings more carefully. Wesley assumed that this was what the control meant by "Please secure your posture." He wished he would have been lying in bed or sitting in a stable reclining chair. His body was contorted into a funny position with his mouth open against his knee.

After several minutes of sitting there, Wesley began to panic. He was completely paralyzed. What if something had gone wrong? What if he was supposed to do something to prevent paralysis? He was scared he would be in this condition forever.

Then his sense of sound clicked off. He was deaf.

Then the color in his vision disappeared. He was color blind. Everything was shades of gray.

Then his vision clicked off completely, and all that was left was black.

He assumed his consciousness was the last to go.

🕹 👾 🕹

It seemed like he was waiting in the black for a very long time. Nothing was happening. He wondered if this was what it would be like to be in a coma. He wondered if he had left his front door unlocked.

Then, out of the black, Wesley saw large black letters in front of him:

The letters spelled: Loading. Please wait.

Beneath the words, a bar stretched slowly to the right with a counter to show how much loading time there was left. Wesley was already getting bored. Waiting for games to load was the main reason why he stopped playing them.

Once it was finished loading, the Cybernetrix logo flashed across his vision. Then some music slowly became audible. It was the Cybernetrix theme song. When the music ended, the logo disappeared and Wesley was able to move his eyes. His senses were being downloaded into the system one sense at a time. He could tell that his motor functions were in the download phase.

He was standing on a glowing white platform about twenty feet in diameter. Beyond the platform was silent television static. Once his movement came to him, he lifted his hands up to his face. They were glowing green. Bright neon green lines coiled through his flesh like circuits. He was wearing white armor pads that seemed as light as Tupperware and reflected the neon light.

As his sense of touch came to him, he could feel the warmth of his green glowing circuits. He could feel the energy pulsing through them. He rubbed his head and felt a smooth helmet.

He was exactly like Tron. Well... he was more like a B-movie rip-off version of Tron. He was a... Cybernetron?

His footsteps made static tapping noises as he stepped in a circle on the platform. He couldn't believe how real it all felt.

Don was right, Wesley thought, this truly does feel like I'm in a completely new world.

Not only did he feel like he was in a new world, he felt like he was in a completely new body. Not a human body, but some kind of electro-human body. It was a wondrous feeling.

Once Wesley was completely downloaded into the 'netrix, the floor lit up and he was transported through a vortex tunnel at the speed of light.

Wesley arrived in a pink and blue neon room, the size of a restaurant. It was some kind of Tron-world lounge, with glowing couches and bar stools and cocktail tables. There were some cybertronetic people chatting nearby. A green-glowing man and a violet-glowing female were standing near a cocktail table. The female was leaning on the translucent pink table with her elbow, while resting her arm on the curve of her hip. On one of the couches, there was a violet-glowing female and a violet-glowing male with a green-glowing male.

"Wes?" one of the green-glowing males called.

Wesley looked over to him. It was Don Conway's voice.

"You actually made it!" Don said. "Wunderbar!"

"Hi," Wesley said.

Wesley didn't recognize Don right away. He wasn't in the shape of a short fat man anymore. He was in a tall, muscle-bound, cybernetronic body that would have intimidated even Chuck Nelson. On top of the massive body, he still had the same plump round face, though, with the little mustache and the little glasses. His mustache and glasses also glowed with green neon light.

"Everybody, come meet the new guy," Don said.

The other cybernetronic people gathered around him.

"This is Wes," Don said.

"Wesley," Wesley said.

"Hi, Wes!" a violet-glowing woman cried to Wesley.

"Let me introduce everyone," Don said. "This is Steve Bowser."

An African-American violet-colored cybernetronic man stepped forward. "How's it going?"

Wesley shook his hand.

"Steve works at WinCorp, too, in the accounting department," Don said. Then he turned to one of the violet-colored females. "This is Amy. She used to be the in-charge in our apartment. I mentioned her earlier today, remember? She works downstairs now."

"Hi, Wes!" Amy cried. She was a very thin, petite girl. She looked very young, practically a teenager.

"And then there's these two," Don said. He pointed at the green-colored man first. He was a little older than Wesley with piercing black eyes and a broad chin. "This is Max88."

"A pleasure," said the man.

"And this is Xiva23," Don said, pointing to the curvy violet-colored girl.

"Nice to meet you," Xiva said. She shook Wesley's hand vertically, as if she wanted him to kiss her knuckles, and bowed. Wesley bowed back.

Xiva's voice was soft yet strong and confident, like a Japanese business man. She also had a beautiful face with smooth cheeks, large purple eyes, and a heart-shaped mouth with full fleshy lips. She didn't smile at Wesley, but there was something in her eyes that attracted his attention. He couldn't look away from her.

"It's Wes' first time," Don said.

"How exciting!" Amy cried.

"Oh, my God," said Steve. "You are going to die once you see everything that can be done here."

"It's really fun!" Amy cried, waving her twiggy arms around to create tracers of purple light. "Insanely fun! You might as well call in sick for the next month, because you're not going to want to do anything else but play this game."

"It's crazy," Wesley said. "I still don't believe it's this real."

Steve and Amy nodded their heads and smiled at Wesley for a while, remembering back to when they were newbies and how exciting it was for them.

"You know you could have chosen any form that you wanted, Wes," Don said. "You look exactly like you did in real life. It's more fun to change things up. You can have any body you want."

"I don't need to do that," Wesley said.

"Do you know how?" Don asked.

"No," Wesley said.

"All of your controls are on your power disc," Don said. He

35

removed the green-glowing Frisbee disc from Wesley's back.

Wesley examined the disc. There were different buttons on it.

"To bring up the options menu, you click this button," Don said, clicking the button.

A green holographic menu opened up in the air two feet above the Frisbee. Don clicked the scroll down buttons to show Wesley what he could do. "This is how you control pretty much everything. Use this if you want to exit the game or save your place in a game or if you want to change your appearance or if you want to alter the sound settings or change which team you're on—purple or green—or if you want to see who is logged in on other platforms. You can send emails, check email, log on to the internet, make calls to other people within the game or even to people in the real world. Heck, if they would let me I could do my whole job from here."

Wesley was amazed.

"We're at the beginning of a whole new age, I tell you. A whole new age."

They hung out in the lounge area of platform 023X for a while, just chatting. Amy and Steve seemed to be a couple. They were very friendly with each other and wrapped themselves around each other a lot. Don was nearby, wiggling his electro-mustache at them as they laughed and joked about events in the game that Wesley didn't understand. Max and Xiva were playing a game of holographic chess on one of the cocktail tables.

Wesley walked around the room, getting accustomed to this new world. It was odd to be without a sense of smell or taste, but his maneuverability seemed improved. He felt lighter on his feet, more agile. It was like the gravity was different. The whole experience was really exciting to Wesley. He forgot all about his depressing real world life. Just sitting down on a glowing blue sofa and standing up again was fun for Wesley. It was all new to him, like he was reborn and just experiencing life for the first time.

After he was finished exploring the room, Wesley went over to Don but he was busy checking his email. Amy and Steve seemed to be having a private conversation, so he went over to watch Max and Xiva's chess game. Wesley couldn't tell who was winning, but Xiva had a very confident look on her face.

Wesley thought Xiva was really cute. He couldn't take his eyes off of her. Every facial expression she made caused Wesley to swoon a little. His insides were tingling. Though she was very feminine in her physique and posture, her attitude seemed more masculine than feminine. Wesley hoped she wasn't a Japanese business man in real life.

"Let's go," Don said, as he closed his email.

"What're we playing?" Steve asked.

"Lazerbikes," Don said.

"We should show Wes around the promenade first!" Amy cried.

"I want to play lazerbikes," Don said. "That's the best thing."

"We can play lazerbikes all night after we show him the promenade," Amy cried.

"Let's just take a short jump to the promenade's central court for a few minutes and then transport right to the game grid from there," Steve said.

"Okay," Don said. "As long as we don't take too long."

The six of them stepped up onto the transport pad and beamed across the 'netrix to the promenade, which was the center of the virtual world. It was an enormous cityscape of neon lights. It was perhaps as big as Portland's city center, with tall buildings made of blue light, the sky a pink vortex.

Don pointed out the largest building in the square and said, "That is the Overlord Program building."

Wesley saw a large building lit with red and yellow lasers.

"It is the program that controls all of Cybernetrix," Don said. "It is like the god of the game, the evil dictator that oppresses the Cybernetrons."

Wesley wondered if the Overlord Program looked like the Master Control Program in Tron. He wondered if he would someday be able to fight him by throwing a Frisbee at a row of circling shields.

Crowds of cybernetronic people moved through the streets. All of them were either violet or green, though there were a few people that were yellow and there was one person who was orange.

"Who are the yellow people?" Wesley asked.

"They are the admins," Don said. "They work for Atari and make sure the game is going smoothly from within. They can answer questions if you need help."

"I want their job!" Amy cried, wiggling her purple butt lights at Don.

Amy doesn't have very large breasts, Wesley thought, but she's got a perfect little butt.

"What about the orange people?" Wesley asked.

"Orange people?" Steve asked.

"You see an orange person?" Amy cried. "Where?"

"Up ahead," Wesley said. "In that arena thing."

"He's actually playing?" Don cried.

"Who?" Steve asked.

"What?" Wesley asked.

"Omega," Xiva said.

"Really?" Steve said.

"Who's Omega?" Wesley asked.

"Omega is the master of games," Xiva told Wesley.

Wesley felt like he was getting sucked into Xiva's eyes as she spoke to him.

"Let's go see it," Don said, "before it's over."

They all sprinted closer to the arena. They ran past a café with outdoor seating, where people drank cups of glowing blue fluid. It was like they were drinking tea, but it was a kind of electric tea. While the people took sips of the fluid, their circuit lights glowed brighter for short bursts. Wesley wondered why they would be drinking anything in the Cybernetrix. Wesley thought: since they have no sense of taste and since none of this is real, what possible reason could they have for drinking it? Perhaps it's just for fun.

Don pushed his way through the crowd of glowing cyber-netrons toward the stage. His companions followed. Omega's helmet was longer than a normal cybernetron's helmet and covered up most of his face. It also had horns. His skin glowed with dark orange circuitry. His power disc was serrated around the edges like a circular saw.

Omega stood in the middle of the stage, looking out over the crowd of Users and waiting for the match to begin.

"He is the Overlord's champion," Don told Wesley. "The toughest enemy in the game."

"You hardly ever see him!" Amy cried.

Don said, "Only top players can challenge Omega. You only get one shot to play him. If you fail you lose all your game points and have to start over. If you beat him you get to become a lord of Cybernetrix. Lords are supposed to be able to get a ton of privileges that other Users don't have. You can fly, for instance, and you can get your own hover tank. I think you also have a lot more options for customizing your look. There's a lot you can do if you become a lord. I don't even know all the perks."

"But nobody has beaten Omega before," Xiva said.

"Yeah," Don said. "He's nearly unbeatable."

While standing in the crowd waiting for the match to begin, Wesley inched toward Xiva secretly. For some reason, he found himself wanting to be closer to her. He felt the warmth of her violet light circuits radiating out of her. He wondered what it would feel like to embrace her, to have her electric body pressed against him.

Xiva noticed Wesley inching closer to her. She turned and looked him in the eyes, and Wesley quickly stepped back. Xiva watched him for a while, examining him, without saying a word. It was an uncomfortable silence.

Wesley didn't know what to do so he said, "Have you ever seen Omega fight?"

"Three times," Xiva said. "They aren't very fun to watch."

"Why?" Wesley said.

"See for yourself," Xiva said, pointing at the stage right as the match began.

It was over in two seconds. The challenger, a purple Korean cybernetron, threw his power disc at Omega like a bullet, but Omega's power disk knocked the Frisbee out of the air and hit the Korean in the chest, causing him to explode into a cloud of neon violet pixels.

The crowd cheered for Omega.

"He's too good," Xiva said.

"I see what you mean," Wesley said.

Wesley smiled at her.

She didn't smile back.

They left the promenade and teleported to a free game grid to play Lazerbike Fight. Don, Wesley, and Max would be one team, the green team, and Xiva, Steve, and Amy their purple opponents.

"The object of the game is to force your opponents to crash into the walls," Don told Wesley. "You create lazer-walls as you drive and you'll want to use them to trap your opponents."

"But you can also use their walls against them," Steve said.

"I don't know what you mean," Wesley said. "Walls?"

"Didn't you see Tron?" Don asked.

"Yeah," Wesley said.

"And you don't remember the lightcycles?" Amy cried.

"The lazerbikes are basically the same thing as the lightcycles from Tron," Don said.

"Yeah, I remember those motorcycle things," Wesley said.

"And do you remember the jet-walls that came out of them?" Don asked.

"Maybe," Wesley said.

"Let's just play," Max said in an annoyed voice.

Max had been waiting quietly all night, but his patience had just run out.

"Yeah, come on," Xiva said. "He'll learn as he plays."

Each team stood on opposite sides of the game grid. The neon-blue grid was miles wide and miles high. Above, Wesley could see the ceiling was more like a computerized sky. It was another grid, only it was neon red instead of blue.

Don taught Wesley how to get into lazerbike mode. He brought up the menu on Wesley's power disc, highlighted the item "Lazerbike Mode" and told him to press enter. Once he pressed enter, a sheet of green energy burst from the power disc. It enveloped him and quickly mutated into the shape of a lazerbike around him. Don and Max went into Lazerbike mode soon afterward. They revved their engines, ready to do battle.

On the other end of the grid, three purple lazerbikes revved their engines back at them.

"Let's go!" Don yelled, and all the lazerbikes entered the game grid, except for Wesley's.

Wesley didn't know how to control it yet. He watched as Don's lazerbike sped off into the distance, leaving a thin neon green wall like a trail. Wesley examined his controls. His power disc had been converted into some kind of steering wheel. But he couldn't find the gas.

"Come on, Wes!" Don shouted through the intercom that was emitting through his power disc. "Get in the game!"

"How do I get going?" Wesley said.

"Oh, brother... " Max said.

"Hit the gas," Don said. "Push off with your feet."

Wesley realized there was a pedal under his heels. He was leaning in a forward position, with his feet behind him, so he didn't notice the pedal before.

Pressing down on the pedal just once blasted him off into the game grid. The lazerbike only had one speed: fast. He couldn't slow down, speed up, or stop, unless he crashed.

Turning the wheel only slightly caused him to do an immediate 90 degree turn. He turned right, then left, then right, then left, then right, then left, imagining that the lazer-wall behind him was beginning to look a lot like stairs.

Ahead of him, Wesley could see green and violet walls being formed across the horizon. There was a green explosion and Max cried out through the intercom, then he was silent.

"Wes, where are you?" Don called. "I need you,"

"I'm coming," Wesley called.

Wesley came speeding forward toward the maze of neon walls. He saw a purple explosion in the distance.

"Yeehaw!" Don cried. "Got one!"

Wesley wasn't sure what was going on up there. He was too far back. He kept going forward until he saw the other lazerbikes. A green lazerbike was crossing Wesley's path up ahead, cutting off Wesley's entire view of the game grid.

"Sorry, Wes," Don said. "I blocked you off. Turn left."

Wesley turned left and followed the green wall on his right.

Out of nowhere, a purple wall formed across Wesley's view and the green lazerbike crashed into it. Don was out of the game. It was just Wesley and two of the purple players.

Before Wesley knew what was going on, there were purple bikes flying past him on his left side and behind him. They boxed him in. He thought that they might have accidentally left a tiny opening for him to escape through, but after making three turns in order to find an exit from the box Wesley realized that he had just trapped himself inside of a smaller box of his own creation and then he crashed into one of his own walls. His senses went black and he soon found himself rematerializing on the platform outside of the game grid. Don, Max, and Steve were shaking their heads at Wesley's performance.

The match went to the purple team.

Wesley said, "It's my first time, what did you expect?"

They played Lazerbike Fight all night long. Wesley got better the more he played. The better he got, the more fun it became. He was still the worst rider on the game grid, but it was the most excitement he'd had since Disneyland when he was eight years old.

Most of the matches, Wesley died first. He spent most of his time waiting on the platform, which they had nicknamed "the deathbox," hanging out with the other dead players. He wished Xiva died more often so that he could get to know her better, but she was one of the best players and rarely died.

Xiva was the one who killed Wesley the most. The other players took it easy on Wesley, because he's the newbie, but Xiva just saw him as easy-pickings. She always seemed to target him first. Wesley wondered if she was sadistic. He wondered if she enjoyed the idea of trapping him within her walls until he exploded. Maybe she just took the game too seriously. Maybe she thought Wesley would be offended if she took it easy on him.

They played all the way until morning. Don explained that

they didn't need to sleep when playing Cybernetrix, because their bodies at home were already essentially sleeping. It wasn't exactly the same as real sleeping. The doctors called it "yellow sleep" which was kind of like sleeping without ever reaching REM sleep. Don said that it wasn't good to replace sleep with playing Cybernetrix, but if you play Cybernetrix all the time you won't need to sleep very much. Then Don admitted that he hadn't had a real night's sleep all year.

No wonder why Don is so obsessed with this game, Wesley thought. If you were living inside this world during all of your free time, including in your sleep, there's probably nothing else you'd care to talk about either.

Wesley was sitting in the deathbox and checked the time on his power disc. The time said 5:40 a.m. Xiva had finally died near the beginning of a match, at the same time as Wesley. They crashed into each other. She looked really tired. Even though her body was asleep in the real world, the yellow sleep must not have been cutting it for her. With how good she was at the lazerbikes, she must have played a lot of this game. Wesley wondered if it had been years since she slept last. He, on the other hand, was not tired or exhausted at all. Things like tiredness, pains, and discomfort didn't seem to exist in the Cybernetrix world.

But Xiva sure looked tired. Her violet circuits weren't glowing very brightly. Without saying a word to Wesley, she sat down next to him on the platform and leaned her weight against his side. She needed to use him for a chair.

"Are you alright?" Wesley asked her, but she didn't respond.

She placed her head on his shoulder and closed her eyes. Her smooth helmet found a comfortable place within the crook of his neck. He liked the feeling of her helmet against his skin. The helmet was not removable, so it was basically like a bald head. For some reason, he liked the idea of her smooth bald head pressed against his neck.

He kind of liked the way some girls looked when they had bald heads. It's commonly known as a masculine thing, but Wesley believed a bald head on a girl could be extremely feminine. Without hair, a woman was able to show off her face and ears, she could expose her entire neck. Wesley believed that the neck was one of the most beautiful parts of the female body. He thought it was a shame that most women covered up their necks with long hair or necklaces or turtle neck sweaters.

Wesley soaked in the sensation of Xiva's weight against his body. He could feel not only the warmth, but a pulsing of energy flowing through her system. Her flesh vibrated slightly, like the purr of a cat. Wesley's body purred back in response, but Wesley didn't understand how he was generating the purrs.

Wesley began to wonder if Xiva was only pretending to be tired so she could lean against him like this. He hoped she had a crush on him, just as he had one on her. After leaning against Wesley for a while, Xiva's circuits began to glow brighter again. Once they were at full glow, she stood up and was ready to play again. His circuits were not glowing quite as brightly anymore.

CHAPTER THREE
ELECTRIC TEA

Wesley was actually able to get to work early that day, since he had been hanging out with co-workers all night and into the morning. His spirits were up after meeting Xiva and having such a fun time with Cybernetrix, but his body felt like hell from being contorted into a pretzel all night. His neck felt like it was on sideways. His back felt like it was broken in a dozen places.

The worst part was that gravity seemed so much heavier now, in the real world. He had gotten used to the lighter gravity in the Cybernetrix. His sense of smell was also really strong, because he had gotten used to not using that sense.

Wesley thought it was crazy how a single night of gameplay would result in a completely different perspective on reality. Unfortunately, he found his sense of smell much less appealing than he used to. Everything he smelled seemed to have a horrible stench that assaulted his senses. Even perfumes and food had a rottenness to them that Wesley had never noticed before. Having a strong sense of smell was not a good thing.

Rickman called Wesley into his office first thing.

"Hey, my man, crazy hat day isn't until Friday!" Rickman said with a faux smile, laughing.

He pointed at Wesley's hair and Wesley realized that it was sticking straight up. Wesley guessed that Rickman was referring to his hair as if it was a crazy hat, so he smoothed down the section of hair that was sticking up.

"What happened to you?" Rickman told Wesley, chuckling. "Were you playing Cybernetrix all night or something?"

"Yeah," Wesley said.

Rickman's smile faded.

"Serious?" Rickman said. "I had no idea you were a Cybernetrix player. If I had I wouldn't have hired you."

"What do you mean?" Wesley asked. "I tried it for the first time last night. What is wrong with it?"

"It's a horrible game," Rickman said. "I know. I've played it. Several times. It seems like all fun and games at first, but there's more to it than that. It's a disgusting place. It's worse than any drug on the streets. It will change you."

"Is it illegal?" Wesley said.

"No, it's not illegal, yet," Rickman said. "It sure should be. It's ruining our youth. It's like a drug. The more you play the less you'll be able to stop. The more you play the more your body will become dependent on the game. You've got to promise me that you'll never play it again."

"But I don't get it," Wesley said. "What exactly is so wrong about it?"

"Lots of things. Far more than I'm willing to list." Rickman shut the door to his office and chugged at his coffee as if it were bourbon and he was trying to get drunk fast. "There's no proof of this, but I believe they put some kind of chemical into your brain when you play so that you'll never want to leave the game world. I believe this because I used to play all the time and once I quit—so that I could spend more time with my wife—I started to get withdrawals. All I could think about was playing Cybernetrix again. I had to get professional help. I nearly lost my wife and my job. It is a serious problem in this country."

"Anything in excess will be bad for you," Wesley said.

"I agree with you there," Rickman said, "but with Cybernetrix there's only excess. You can't just do it a little at a time. Once you start you can't stop until every moment of your life is spent within the computer world. You start to hate reality. Only the world in that game will start to mean something to you."

Rickman took another chug. "You've got to promise me you will quit now. Pick up another hobby immediately. Try writing or drawing or playing an instrument. Whatever happened to young people doing those types of things in their free time? We've got too many people in this office hooked on the game already. We don't need any more."

Wesley nodded. "I understand."

"Good," Rickman said. "Now, how far did you get with training yesterday?"

A nerve rippled through Wesley's spine. He didn't want to admit to Rickman that he did absolutely nothing yesterday, but he knew it would be a mistake to say he watched those videos when he really didn't.

"It didn't go too well," Wesley said.

"Why's that?" Rickman said, faking a sad expression. It was the same expression that he would have used if Wesley had told him that his dog had just died.

"Chuck spent all day looking for those training tapes," Wesley said, calmly. "But he couldn't find them, so I mostly just acquainted myself with the building and my new co-workers."

"That's too bad," Rickman said. "At least it wasn't a complete waste of a day, though. Good job."

Wesley had told him the right lie. He just told his boss right to his face that all he did was walk around the office and chit-chat with people, but he did it in a way that made him come off as if he'd done a good job rather than absolutely nothing.

Wesley was proud of himself. Yesterday, there was no way he would have been able to lie to Rickman like that. He would have been too scared. Playing Cybernetrix did seem to be changing Wesley, but only for the better. He was more confident and happy. His worries didn't seem to matter anymore.

Rickman's wrong about Cybernetrix, Wesley thought. There's plenty of good that can come out of that game.

Rickman was going to be in meetings all day again, but he told Wesley to make sure Chuck got him those training tapes. He told him to try asking Mrs. Gensen if Chuck couldn't find them again. He said she always seemed to know where everything was in the office.

Neither Don nor Chuck were in their cubicles when Wesley arrived, so he decided to go look for one of them. He swung by Shelly's desk. Shelly's bangs weren't as puffy as they were the day before, but they were longer now and went all the way down past her eyebrows. She looked up at Wesley and then darted her eyes back to her paper nervously as he approached her. She didn't know that he was coming to speak with her.

"Have you seen Chuck today?" Wesley asked her.

She looked up at Wesley with a surprised look as if she didn't notice him there, even though they made eye contact only a second before.

"Ah—" she began with a wide mouth, but then she just shook her head instead of giving a reply.

"Thanks," Wesley said.

Something forced him to fake-smile at her and blink.

She smiled back with a blush and darted her eyes back onto her paper. Her smile was genuine, though. It was a nervous smile, but it wasn't fake. Wesley was glad he faked a smile for her.

Perhaps it's good to fake smiles now and again to make the office environment more friendly, Wesley thought. And perhaps the people who believe that to be true end up smiling so much that their smile becomes meaningless and empty. Like Rickman.

Wesley peeked into the break room to see if either Chuck or Don were in there. A bunch of people were inside drinking coffee, chatting or reading newspapers. They were having their pre-work coffee break.

"Hey, it's Wes!" cried a woman in the break room.

Wesley looked over and saw two people excitedly waving at him. One was a morbidly obese woman with a platinum blond Eurythmics hairstyle. The other was a skinny Jewish man with thick glasses.

She excitedly beckoned him to come to them.

"Get over here!" cried the woman.

Wesley walked slowly and hesitantly over to them.

"It's us!" cried the obese woman. "Steve and Amy!"

Wesley's facial expression was loudly saying, *huh?*

"From last night!" she cried. "You don't recognize us?"

Then she laughed.

Of course he didn't recognize them. Amy was a cute little teenaged girl in the game, but a middle-aged mammoth of a woman in real life. Steve was a handsome black man in the game, but in real life he was a scrawny Jewish guy with thick glasses and braces.

"We don't use our real image in the game like you do," she cried.

"It's more fun to be someone different," Steve said.

Wesley started to become worried about what Xiva looked like in real life. Was she a morbidly obese middle-aged woman like Amy in real life? Or was she actually a Japanese business man, as her personality suggested? He really liked Xiva and hated the idea that she was not exactly like that in real life.

"Are you going to play again tonight?" Amy asked.

"Yeah," said Wesley. "I'm on the 7-day-trial and want to make the most of it. I won't be able to afford it for a long time after that."

"You don't have to worry about that," Steve said. "The monthly charge will come in on your cell phone bill, which you don't necessarily have to pay on time. You'll get enough money from this job soon enough to pay it back."

"I guess you're right," Wesley said.

"You picked up Lazerbike Fight pretty fast!" Amy cried,

bouncing the massive collection of fat on her hips (which resembled an inner tube around her midsection) from side to side as she spoke. "A few more times and you'll be as good as any of us!"

"It was really fun," Wesley said. "What other games can you play in Cybernetrix?"

"There's Discs of Death," Steve said. "I like that one best, personally, but nobody else does. That's the one where you throw your power discs at the opponents to knock them out of the game until there's only one team left."

"Don doesn't like it because it reminds him of dodgeball," Amy said. "He has bad memories of playing dodgeball, so he rarely ever lets us play it."

"There's also Voltro Jai Alai," Steve said. "It's really hard, though."

"Are you afraid of heights?" Amy cried.

"Kind of," Wesley said.

"So am I," Amy cried. "You don't want to play the Jai Alai game if you're afraid of heights. If you lose, it takes a long period of free-falling before you de-res. I can't stand that feeling. It's not real, of course, but it feels terrible. Like when you fall off of a cliff in your dreams."

"It's pretty difficult, too," Steve said. "We rarely play it."

"Hover Tanks is fun though!" Amy cried.

"Do you remember the game Space Paranoids in the movie Tron?" Steve said.

"I don't think so," Wesley said.

"You basically drive a robo-tank through a vector maze and shoot at the Hover Tanks that come at you," Steve said. "It's the funnest game to play when you just want to play something by yourself."

"It's also fun to play with two people!" Amy cried. "Because one person can steer and one can shoot."

"There's a ton of other things that you can do, though," Steve said. "The games are just a tiny part of Cybernetrix."

"It seemed like it," Wesley said.

"The more you play the more you'll understand that

Cybernetrix has unlimited possibilities for entertainment," Steve said. "You can do almost anything in that world as you can in this one."

"Only better!" Amy cried, then she laughed.

Wesley's heightened sense of smell was assaulted by a wave of horrid oyster-breath from Amy when she laughed. It almost made him sick. He couldn't believe that cute little girl in the game was really just this smelly fat woman in front of him.

Wesley was so disgusted by Amy that he became really concerned about what Xiva was like in real life. If she was different in real life he had to know.

"Do you know Xiva personally?" Wesley asked Amy and Steve. "Outside of the game?"

"What do you mean?" Steve asked.

"I was wondering if she looked like that in real life," Wesley said. "Is she from Portland?"

"You're kidding, right?" Amy cried.

"Wes," Steve said with a concerned face. "You know she's just a bot, right?"

Wesley was confused.

"She's an AI program," Steve continued. "She doesn't really exist."

The two of them burst into laughter.

Wesley's face drooped. At first, he didn't believe him. He thought they were pulling his leg. Then he remembered that they called her Xiva23. That was the type of name they would give to a bot. Wesley originally thought that it was just a screen name. He couldn't understand how she could possibly be a part of the game world.

Amy and Steve could tell that this news was devastating Wesley, which made it all the funnier to them.

"You have a crush on one of the robots!" Amy cried. "Don

has got to hear this! I can't believe it!"

"Max and Xiva are just computer-generated personalities," Steve told Wesley. "We only use them so that we can have more players in our games."

Wesley didn't know what to say. He was embarrassed and felt sick.

"I didn't know," Wesley said.

"I never heard of such a thing!" Amy cried.

"I need to go find Chuck," Wesley said, softly.

He backed away from them.

"Don't go," Amy cried. "I'm not mocking you. I think it's cute!"

"I've got to go," Wesley said.

"See you tonight!" Steve called, as Wesley was exiting the break room.

👾 👾 👾

Wesley was heartbroken by this news. He didn't like how his day was going anymore. Reality had a way of stomping on Wesley's happiness lately. He wished he could have kept things the way they were last night, while he was in the fantasy world. He preferred Amy as the cute girl and Steve as the black man, and he wished he still believed Xiva was a real human being and not some computer generated image programmed to act in a certain way.

Wesley wandered through the office. He pretended like he was looking for Chuck Nelson, but he was really just trying to walk off his embarrassment. Amy worked downstairs so luckily he wouldn't have to see her again for the rest of the day. He hoped he would never have to see her in real life ever again.

While walking by a cubicle, he saw a man bringing a cup of glowing blue light up to his lips. It was like the electric tea from Cybernetrix. Wesley stepped back to get a better look at the fluid, but the man had tipped the cup to drink and Wesley could no longer see what was inside. The man, a bulky old man with a black unibrow and a crusty red face covered in birthmarks, gave Wesley a dirty look. Wesley decided to move away from him before he asked him what he was doing there.

It couldn't have been electric tea, Wesley thought. That stuff only exists in the Cybernetrix world.

Chuck and Don were both outside, smoking and having a conversation, avoiding work. Don, of course, couldn't have a conversation about anything except Cybernetrix. Wesley squeezed next to them to listen in.

"I'm telling you, it would change your life," Don told Chuck.

"Yeah, I believe you," Chuck said. "I'd end up as fat and lonely as you."

"Actually, I've lost fifty pounds since I've been playing," Don said. "I've also got more friends then ever."

"All a bunch of losers," Chuck said.

"All types of people from all over the world play the game," Don said. "There are tons of people just like you that play it. I'm telling you, you've got to give it a shot at least once."

Don spotted Wesley over Chuck's shoulder.

"Look at Wes," Don said. "Just yesterday he wasn't interested in it but then tried it last night and it blew him away. Right, Wes?"

Chuck and Don turned to Wesley.

"It's unbelievable," Wesley said.

"I'm sure throwing some Frisbees around is great and all," Chuck said, "but I'd rather get laid."

Chuck took a drag off of his cigarette and continued, "I mean, when's the last time you got laid, Don? You've probably been in geek oblivion for so long that you don't even know what sex is anymore."

"Are you kidding!" Don said. "I get laid all the time."

"Bullshit," Chuck said. "You couldn't get laid even if you paid for it."

"Seriously," Don said. "I can get laid any time I want."

"How?" Chuck said.

"In the game," Don said. "The sex is what Cybernetrix is most popular for."

"You can have sex in the game?" Chuck laughed.

"Yeah, of course," Don said. "I told you before, you can feel everything in the game. Even sexual pleasure. And since it all happens within a virtual world, it is all 100% safe sex. There's a whole sexual revolution going on in the 'netrix. The underground sex scene is enormous. You can look like whatever you want, so even the most fattest, ugliest people can get laid. Anyone can have sex with anyone. If you don't like the way they look you can change their appearance for them so they can meet your taste in sexual partner."

Chuck's mouth was wide open. He couldn't believe his ears.

"You've got to be shitting me," Chuck said.

"Not at all," Don said. "It's the honest to God truth. And I'm telling you, you haven't had sex until you've had Tron sex. It's as simple as that."

"You mean for $200 a month I could be getting all the pussy I want?" Chuck asked. "And I can turn any fat hairy cow into a bodacious blond with gigantor hooters? And the girls put out no questions asked?"

"Well, you can't make her blond," Don said. "Everyone wears helmets so you don't see their hair. But you can make her breasts as big as watermelons. It's all completely safe and if you change the way you look your identity is completely private."

"I am so there!" Chuck said. Then he gave Wesley a high-five.

Chuck tossed his cigarette and headed for the door.

"We meet on platform 023X at 7pm every night," Don said. "If you want us to show you around."

"I don't want to play with you losers," Chuck said as he entered the building. "I'll figure it out myself."

Wesley stood there and watched Don smoke his cigarette and raise his eyebrows up and down. Chuck left before Wesley was able to ask him about those training videos.

👾 👾 👾

The rest of the day was exactly as it was the day before. Chuck was nowhere to be seen and Wesley spent his time chatting with Don about Cybernetrix.

Wesley didn't care if he was goofing off. It was Chuck's fault. All he cared about was going home and logging back into the Cybernetrix world.

CHAPTER FOUR:
ELECTRO-SEX UNDERGROUND

Wesley didn't bother eating or taking off his work clothes when he got home. He went straight for the Cybernetrix hardware. This time he set himself up on the bed so that he wouldn't be so sore the next morning. Then he logged in.

It wasn't as frightening being uploaded into the system this time. It didn't seem to take as long, either. It wasn't even six o'clock yet, so he was the first person on the platform. Wesley wondered if there was an infinite number of platforms. He wondered if all you had to do was sign up for one and you'd have it forever.

Wesley spent his time investigating the room. He wondered how he could play holographic chess like the bots were doing the day before. Examining one of the cocktail tables, he discovered a small control panel and figured out how to bring up an options menu similar to the one on his power disc. The menu listed all of the holographic games you could play. There was chess, checkers, backgammon, several card games, stratego, parcheesi, Chinese checkers, mahjong, and tiddlywinks. There weren't any one-player games, so Wesley chose tiddlywinks just because he thought it was funny.

Pink holograms issued out of the cocktail table and created some translucent tiddlywinks. Wesley picked up a tiddlywink head. He could see through it like glass, and it felt like it was made of pure energy, but he was able to hold it in his hand. When he tossed the piece away from the table, it disappeared before it hit the floor and reappeared on the table.

Wesley selected chess on the options menu. The tiddlywinks disappeared from the table and a chess set appeared. He selected a card game, Texas hold 'em poker, and selected the two player option. Stacks of neon blue, green, and pink chips appeared on each side of the table and two cards, a nine of clubs and a two of hearts, appeared in his hand. He examined the cards. They looked like sheets of green energy that he could see through, but when he turned the card around it was no longer translucent.

Weird, Wesley thought. They put a lot of detail into this game.

After a while, Wesley got bored of hanging out by himself and wished he would have somebody to play one of these games with.

He didn't want to try to go play with other users, though. He wondered if he could play the computer. Maybe he could play a bot.

There was a control console for the platform. Wesley inspected it. It mostly seemed like teleportation controls. He scrolled down the menu and found other options, like Room Settings, which included Lighting, Dimensions, Play Music, Change Style, and Features. At the bottom of the list there was the option: Call Player. Wesley selected that. The list then read Invite User and Invite Bot.

"Jackpot," Wesley said.

He selected Invite Bot.

An enormous list of available bot names appeared. There were hundreds of them. Wesley scrolled through all of the Aarons and Adrics. There were a 100 different copies of each bot type, and hundreds of different types of bots. Some bots were more popular than others, while some bots didn't seem popular at all. Wesley scrolled all the way down to the X's.

There were only a few Xiva's available. She seemed to be pretty popular. His eyes lit up when he saw Xiva23 was one of the few available. He selected her right away.

A note popped up that read: Invite Xiva23? Y/N

Wesley clicked Y.

Then the note read: Inviting...

After a few moments of waiting, another note popped up: Invitation Accepted.

Xiva teleported onto the platform. Her hands were resting on her curvy violet-glowing hips, with all of her weight shifted to one side. She watched Wesley as she materialized, giving him a deep stare.

"Hello, Wes," she said.

He was amazed that she knew his name. "You remember me?"

"Of course," she said. "We met just last night."

She shook his hand in the same way she did yesterday by holding it forward as if she wanted him to kiss it. Wesley took her hand and found himself leaning in to kiss her knuckles as she bowed toward him. Her fingers were warm, almost hot, against his lips.

"I didn't realize you could do that," he said.

"We've got really good memories," she said. "Probably better than yours."

"Cool," Wesley said.

She nodded.

"So, do you want to play me?" Xiva asked.

"I guess," Wesley said. "I was just lonely and wanted some company."

"With me?" Xiva asked. "You know there are over 500,000 users in the public chat rooms as we speak. If you want I can teleport you over to one or invite a user to come here."

She walked over to the control panel on the platform and examined the options menu.

"No," Wesley said. "I'd rather hang out with you."

Her expression changed from confidence to curiosity.

"You're better," Wesley said. For some reason he didn't want to tell her that he felt more comfortable hanging around with a bot. He didn't like the idea of meeting some random user.

"Okay," Xiva said. "What do you want to do?"

"Maybe play a card game for a while," Wesley said.

"I prefer chess," Xiva said.

"Okay, we can play chess," Wesley said. "I'm not very good at it, though."

"I'm very good at it," Xiva said.

Xiva destroyed Wesley at chess three times in a row within half an hour. She really liked to win. When she played, she was focused. She didn't speak unless Wesley asked a question. Only he was so shy, even around a bot girl, that he didn't ask many questions. They played mostly in silence. Wesley listened to the sound of her humming electric skin and examined her soft facial features. He noticed that her lips were purple like her eyes and her eyelashes were almost cartoonishly long.

When the others arrived on the platform, petite teenaged Amy giggled at the top of her electro lungs when she saw Wesley hanging out alone with Xiva.

"Look at the lovebirds!" Amy cried.

Don and Steve laughed as well.

"It's the party train coming through!" Don said, wiggling his mustache, tripping off of the platform.

"What took you guys so long?" Wesley asked.

"We went to happy hour after work," Don said. "Sorry, I forgot to invite you."

They were really drunk. Wesley didn't know that you could get drunk before entering the Cybernetrix. He didn't know why you can't feel pain in your real body while in the 'netrix, but can still be drunk. Perhaps the alcohol effects the game just as it effects the mind.

"Chuck was there, though," Don continued. "He said he ditched work and had already bought Cybernetrix and is going to try it out tonight."

"Is he coming here?" Wesley asked.

"He's going to meet us on Platform 069DD," Don said, drunkenly. "In the adult section."

"Adult section?" Wesley said.

"It's where users go for sexual relations," Xiva said. She seemed annoyed that they wanted to go there, but her voice was as calm and contained as ever.

"That's where the orgies happen?" Wesley asked. "Like you mentioned at work today?"

"Yeah," Don said. "It'll blow your mind."

👾 👾 👾

When they were ready to leave, Wesley asked Xiva if she wanted to go with them.

"I don't know," she said. "Do you want me to come with you?"

"Sure," Wesley said.

"I'm not able to have sex," Xiva said.

"I just want you to come along," he said.

"Okay," Xiva said. "If you want."

The other three users could hardly contain their snickers in the background.

👾 👾 👾

They teleported to platform 069DD, which was in the heart of the underground sex scene within Cybernetrix. Only adults were allowed into this section of the world. Children in Cybernetrix had smaller bodies and could never transform into adult forms. These child-sized bodies were locked out of the system if they tried to teleport to the adult section. There was no way a kid could ever get in. Though there were some people, like Amy, who walked around in underage teenage bodies. Since it was just a fantasy, that was okay. But fake bodies that looked under the age of 16 weren't allowed.

Wesley had a look around. The place looked kind of like the inside of a mall, but with a blue laser grid for a ceiling and pink circuits on the walls. There were users of all kinds socializing in the public area, giggling and flirting. Some of them were very intimate, making out in the neon glow, caressing each other's electric light on their flesh. It wasn't the giant orgy Wesley was expecting. It was more like a big mall-sized singles bar.

"When is Chuck coming?" Wesley asked.

"He's probably already here," Don said.

"Let's go have sex! Let's go have sex!" Amy cried. She was like a seventeen year old cartoonish slut on crack. "I call dibs on Wes first!"

"No," Don said to Amy, so that Wesley didn't have to respond. Wesley was afraid that Don wanted first dibs.

"Just kidding, sweetie!" Amy told Wesley. "Maybe I'll have Steve transform into your image and I'll just do him instead."

"And I'll have you transform into him, too!" Steve said, having trouble keeping his balance.

Amy hopped onto Steve's back for a piggyback ride. "And we'll make him watch!"

"They're just joking around," Don told Wesley. "We made it a rule that we're not allowed to sleep with each other, even though we wouldn't recognize each other in custom bodies. Amy and Steve don't even do it, even though they are always all over each other all the time. It's just too awkward in work situations."

Amy and Steve ran away from the platform. They were yelling, "I'm getting laid first!" and "No, I'm getting laid first!" toward the bar area, where people were socializing, flirting, and propositioning each other. Many people in the bar were drinking electric tea like booze.

"If you customize your bodies so much," Wesley said. "How do you know you're not sleeping with people you know?"

"You don't," Don said. "In fact, Amy and I have slept together before without even knowing it. We try to forget about that, though. I hear stories all the time about co-workers accidentally sleeping with each other, brothers and sisters, teachers and students, best friends, worst enemies, all of them having an excellent night of carnal pleasure only to discover later on who they really slept with. Gender seems to be a big issue here. There are a lot of guys that come in the shape of women and a lot of women who come in the shape of guys. You'll probably end up sleeping with guys all the time, thinking they are attractive women, but you just can't worry about it. You have to pretend the fantasy is real or you'll ruin it. Some users will ask the person they're about to have sex with if they could see their true form before they do it, but it's considered a really rude thing to do here. An even worse thing to do is to expose your true form right after you've had sex. There's nothing worse than having sex with a hot young girl only to have her transform into a sixty year old man, laughing his butt off at you. Something similar to that has happened to me before and it was not a fun memory to have, let me tell you."

"I think I might sit this one out tonight," Wesley said. "I've never been comfortable with casual sex."

"Suit yourself," Don said. "You'll come around eventually. Sex really isn't that big of a deal here. It's like a video game. People oppose violence in real life, but enjoy it in video games. Here, people are open to having sex with strangers, even if they would avoid such activities in real life. The only people who don't have sex in Cybernetrix are those who are too young, too scared, or for some reason don't enjoy sex at all. You seem like you come from the too scared variety."

"I don't know," Wesley said. "Maybe I just don't feel like it right now."

"Suit yourself, my friend," Don said. "I'll see you later."

Xiva was off to the side, hiding herself with her arms. She didn't have the same confidence she had while playing the games. She almost looked uncomfortable in this place.

"Are you okay?" Wesley asked Xiva.

"Of course," Xiva said. She didn't smile but she seemed pleased he was talking to her.

"You don't look happy," Wesley said.

"I'm happy," Xiva said, in a monotone voice.

Xiva kept glancing at something in the corner of the room. It was a door that read No Users Allowed.

"What is that?" Wesley asked. "Why aren't users allowed?"

"It's a bot hangout," Xiva said. "Bots go there when they don't want to be around users for a while."

Wesley wondered why bots needed their own hangouts.

"Do you want to go to the bar area?" Wesley asked.

"Do you want me to go?" Xiva asked.

"I want to hang out with you," Wesley said. "If you want to go to the bar we can go to the bar. If you want to stay here we'll stay here."

"Okay," Xiva said. "Let's go to the bar."

👾 👾 👾

Trying to socialize with Xiva in the bar area was a big mistake. People were chatting so loudly, Wesley couldn't hear her very well. They were all flirting very strongly with each other. Some guys didn't seem to have a problem just grabbing a random girl and carrying them off to a private room upstairs like the cavemen used to do.

"Do you want some juice?" Xiva asked Wesley.

"What is that?" Wesley asked.

"Juice," she said, pointing at someone drinking a cup of the electric tea.

"Yeah," he said. "I've been wondering what that was all about."

"I'll go get some for you," she said.

"No," Wesley said, catching her by the arm. "Sit down. I'll get it for us."

She blinked her eyes slowly in a response and slid back down on her bar stool.

Wesley went to the bar and ordered a juice from a bright yellow-lit fat man.

"Can I see your power disc?" asked the admin.

"Power disc?" Wesley said.

"Have you ever ordered the juice before?" asked the admin.

"No," he said. "First time."

"You know it costs real money, right?"

"Really? Just for a fake drink that I can't taste?"

"It's flavorless, but the effects are very pleasant."

"Okay, I'll take two," Wesley said.

The bartender added the cost of the drinks to Wesley's Cybernetrix account on his power disc. Then he poured him two drinks.

"Do bots like these?" Wesley asked.

"You're not giving one to a bot, are you?" asked the admin.

"Yeah, is there something wrong with that?" Wesley asked. "Do they not like it?"

"They like it, sure," the bartender said. "At least, they are programmed to like it. But they aren't real so they don't really enjoy it. They just seem to enjoy it by the reactions they were programmed with."

"Is that all?" Wesley asked. "It doesn't damage them?"

"It doesn't damage them," he said. "It's just a huge waste of money, that's all."

"Okay," Wesley said, grabbing the drinks and stepping away.

The admin called him an idiot once his back was turned.

There was a scream. Wesley dropped the drinks. He looked up to see that it was Xiva23 who was screaming. Some green-glowing asshole had pulled her out of her seat and was groping her. He had her violet breast in his hand and was trying to kiss her neck.

71

Wesley charged at the guy. He kicked him in the side and it broke the man's grasp around Xiva's waist. She elbowed him in the stomach and jumped away, ducking behind Wesley's back.

It was Chuck Nelson.

"Wesley?" Chuck asked. "What the heck?"

"What do think you're doing?" Wesley asked.

"Don't be such a cock-block man," Chuck said, reaching out to grab Xiva's hand.

She gripped Wesley's hips tightly so that Chuck couldn't get his hand all the way around her wrist.

Wesley punched Chuck in the face and kicked him in the balls.

Even though he was now a virtual reality character, Chuck could still feel a good kick in the balls. The fight was separated by two admins. Their yellow circuits were blindingly bright as they pushed Wesley away from Chuck. One of the admins canceled the pain from Chuck's program, so that it felt as if he had never been hit. The other admin stayed between them.

"You," said the admin between them to Chuck, "What were you thinking? She's a bot. You can't have sex with her. She doesn't have the right equipment. And if it had been a real woman, we would have logged you off for the rest of the night."

"And you," the admin told Wesley. "Why are you fighting for her? She's just a bot. She isn't real."

"And you," the admin told Xiva. "Get out of here."

Xiva kept her confident and serious face, but Wesley could see that underneath she was ready to break down and cry. She nodded at the admin and turned around. Then she ran away.

"You're so dead in the real world," Chuck told Wesley.

"Hey," the admin snapped at Chuck. "Settle your differences in the battle arena, not in the real world."

👾 👾 👾

Wesley chased after Xiva. She was heading toward the room marked No Users Allowed.

"Xiva!" Wesley said. "Wait!"

Just before she made it to the door, Wesley caught her by the wrist. She kept pulling forward trying to get away. But once he let go, Xiva didn't escape through the door. Instead, she whipped her body around and grabbed Wesley.

She wrapped her arms around him and squeezed him as tightly to her body as possible and kissed him deeply. Wesley didn't have the time to be shocked. He wrapped his arms around her and kissed her back. Her tongue felt like wet static in his mouth.

Then she pushed him away from her and continued into the user-free zone without looking back.

Wesley didn't know what hit him. He stood there in the river of green and purple users, his mouth still hanging open. It felt like everyone was watching him, but when he turned around he noticed they were all in their own sexual worlds.

He logged off of Cybernetrix and sat at his dinner table in silence for a while. Something had just happened that wasn't supposed to happen. A bot kissed a user with more passion than Wesley ever thought possible.

Even though he wasn't playing Cybernetrix, he was up all night thinking about Xiva. She was acting weird. She gave no indication at all that she had feelings for him. She was very subtle about her feelings, if she even had any feelings at all. She was just a programmed artificial intelligence. He was extremely attracted to her but wasn't expecting a real relationship after he learned she wasn't real. He was just having fun because he felt more comfortable around her than around other girls. She was practice so that he could feel more comfortable around the real thing.

He wasn't awkward around women in college, but he hadn't had a girlfriend since his father died. He didn't want a woman to get in the way of his art, so he completely wrote off the idea of having a girlfriend until after he was a success.

Wesley wondered if he was reading too much into the kiss. She pushed away from him hard and didn't look back. Perhaps she just kissed him to shut him up. Her computer mind probably calculated that it was the action that had the best chance of success.

Lying in bed, unable to sleep. Wesley wasn't going to be able to rest until he figured out what the kiss meant to Xiva23. If it was a randomly generated action that meant nothing, Wesley would be able to live with that. If she meant it, and it sure felt to Wesley like she meant it, then perhaps they could create something real together.

⁂

Wesley couldn't take it anymore. There was not very much time before he was supposed to wake up for work, but he had to see Xiva again. He had to know the truth.

He logged onto Cybernetrix and created his own platform. It asked him what style he wanted it to be. He opted for a smaller cozy room that was centered with a low to the ground square plexiglass coffee table, surrounded by four translucent blue couches. That was pretty much all that could fit in the room, besides a teleportation platform.

On the control panel, Wesley brought up the options menu and selected Call Player and then Invite Bot. There was only one Xiva available at the time. It was Xiva23.

A note popped up that read: Invite Xiva23? Y/N

Wesley clicked Y.

Then the note read: Inviting...

Within a split second, the note said: Invitation Accepted.

Xiva had her eyes on Wesley as she materialized. Before saying a word, she leapt off of the platform and tackled him against the couch. Her hands gripped him tightly, one pressed firmly around his waist and the other tightened around his bicep, tugging him powerfully into her kiss. It was even more passionate than her last kiss. It was as if she was holding back most of her emotion the last time, because they were in public, but now she was able to explode onto him. The same as the first time, Wesley didn't know what had hit him. He kissed her back, awkwardly at first.

He was exhilarated yet confused. He still didn't know if this was real. She was just a character in a game, so she couldn't possibly have feelings for him. He wondered if she was breaking free of her programming and becoming something more, as so many robot characters in science-fiction stories have done before. After a few minutes of contemplating, he decided he didn't care why or how this was happening. He let his mind become blank and let the moment engulf him.

He pulled her closer to him by her smooth hips. His static tongue crackled against hers. She kissed him down his neck, sucking on his veins of green light. She opened her lips and tongued his circuits down his chest. As she licked and sucked on his circuits, his green glow faded slightly. As his light faded, her glow radiated brighter. It felt like she was drinking the energy out of him. He pushed her away and saw his green light covering her tongue. Droplets of green dribbled down her tongue. She was like some kind of cybernetronic vampire, drinking his electric blood.

She licked her lips and then dove at Wesley, holding him in place with all of her strength, wrapping her mouth around his throat, sucking more of the green light from him. Wesley couldn't stop her. He tried to pull himself free, but her fingers were locked tightly around his wrists. She sucked him dry, completely draining him of his battery.

His muscles went limp. He didn't have the strength to stand anymore and collapsed. Even though she wasn't very muscular, Xiva was able to pick him up from the ground with ease. She carried him to the couch and dropped him on his back. His green light was so dim and hers was so bright. Because he was unable to move, Wesley was beginning to panic. He was helpless and completely at her mercy. She could just leave him like that. Without the ability to use his power disc, he couldn't exit the game. If he couldn't exit the game, he'd be trapped in Cybernetrix and if nobody was able to find his body quickly enough he would die of dehydration. He realized that it was possible to be killed by a rogue computer game character.

It only increased his worry when Xiva removed the power disc from his back. He watched as she brought up his menu screen and began tampering with his account. She was accessing his credit card information.

After she was finished with it, she tossed the Frisbee over the couch. She removed her armor and the white cloth wrapped around her waist, revealing her naked cyberflesh. Without her clothing to cover her neon purple flesh circuits, her body shined so brightly that Wesley couldn't look directly at her. She did not remove her helmet, as it was not removable.

Xiva sat down on the couch, leaning over him.

"I have absorbed your essence," she said, rubbing her glowing body at him. "You feel good inside of me."

Wesley watched her caress herself as if the act of absorbing his light was sexually pleasurable to her.

"Your soul is a part of my circuits, now," she said. "I want mine to be a part of yours."

Wesley opened his mouth but he didn't have the energy to speak.

She bent forward and placed her glowing purple breast into his mouth, then told him to suck it. He didn't even have the strength to suck, but he didn't have to. The hot juice from her body was flowing into his mouth and dripping down his throat. He could feel its sparkly oil texture and, strangely, he was able to taste something. There wasn't a flavor to her energy, but it was giving him a strong sensation. It was effecting his nerves and his emotions, like a drug.

As she was feeding him, Xiva writhed above him. She closed her eyes and sucked her upper lip into her mouth.

76

Once his strength returned, he found himself drinking from her breast voluntarily. He wrapped his arms around her back and drank the essence from her. The more he felt the energy inside of him, the more he started to believe that he really was drinking her soul. He could taste her personality and emotions. He could feel what it meant to be Xiva23. Then he realized it was a flavor that he loved. It was simplistic yet was filled with many subtle complexities. She tasted far more human than anyone he has ever known.

After a few moments, he began to crave her. He grabbed her and slurped furiously at her lifeforce, pulling her into him.

"No," she said, wriggling her thighs against his stomach. She pushed off of his chest and away from the couch. Her purple lifeforce was very dim.

She wasn't angry at him for drinking so much of her blood, but she was winded. She leaned against the coffee table and had to regain her strength. While she composed herself, Wesley examined how bright his cyberflesh had become. He was filled with emotion and energy. Even in the outside world, he had never felt so real and alive.

Xiva brought him a cup of electric tea in a wine glass made of yellow light.

"I hope you don't mind," she said. "I took the liberty of ordering us some juice with your user disc. We're going to need it."

Xiva chugged the electric tea and the brightness of her violet circuits returned to her system. Wesley took a sip and his lights soared. It was like an electrical current was sweeping through his body. The fluid intensified his nervous system and gave him what felt like an incredible amount of energy. Xiva sat down next to Wesley and removed his clothes. She began to suck more of his green lifeforce from his body. Wesley held the side of Xiva's smooth helmet and drank the violet energy from her neck. He closed his eyes and could feel Xiva's hand sliding down his stomach toward his penis.

Wesley looked down. He had not seen his cybernetronic penis before. It was without feeling. It was soft, colorless, and unimpressive. When Xiva stroked her hand against it, the cyberpenis sprang to life. It filled itself with bright green circuitry and expanded to seven inches, a decent enough size for Wesley. With the light, came a rush of sensation. The electric tea had made his sense of touch so strong that even the lightest rub to his penis was more powerful than any intercourse he'd ever had in the real world. When Xiva brought his appendage into her wet static mouth, his senses went into overload. All of his nerves became numb everywhere else in his body, focusing all sensation on that one part. It was like his entire body was inside of her mouth. His jaw dropped open and his muscles twitched.

Wesley watched as Xiva used his cyberpenis as a straw to suck the green lifeforce out of his body. They were unable to have sexual intercourse, because bots were not designed with penises or vaginas, but Xiva knew this was something that pleased users. Xiva lowered her mouth all the way down his shaft until it reached her throat, then on the way up she squeezed her lips around his penis and sucked a mouthful of energy out of him, as if she was milking him.

Xiva quickly drained him. Wesley once again lost his strength and found himself unable to move. When Xiva realized this, she pulled Wesley off of the couch by his legs and his helmeted head thumped on the floor. She got on her hands and knees, then crawled over Wesley's body to reach his penis at a new angle.

In sixty-nine position, Wesley could see that Xiva did not have a real vagina but there was a thin crease that somewhat resembled a vagina. He didn't have the strength to lift up his head so he used his tongue. As soon as his tongue pressed against the lips of the false vagina, a large shock of static popped in his mouth. Like how Xiva's touch had brought Wesley's penis into Active Mode, by licking the faux vaginal lips Xiva's vagina came to life. It brightened and opened up. The light inside was blinding. It was a swirling vortex of neon purple. Xiva lowered her crotch into Wesley's face and he drank from her violet pool. Her thighs shivered against his shoulders as he filled himself with her essence.

They exchanged their energies back and forth for several hours, absorbing each others' personalities and feelings. Whenever the intensity of their lights began to fade, they would drink more of the electric tea. Wesley wasn't sure, but he thought he felt his consciousness leaving his body through his penis and go down Xiva's throat, then exit her body through her vagina and re-enter himself.

Xiva's vagina excited and amazed Wesley. It wasn't so much a vagina as it was a gateway to a world of purple light. He was not sure why she had it, even though she was not supposed to have one at all. Perhaps it is not a vagina, but something else completely. Wesley tried to turn Xiva over so they could have vaginal intercourse, but she pushed him away from her and said, "Not yet. Let's save it. I'd like us to be more like strangers for a while." Wesley agreed.

When Wesley orgasmed, Xiva pulled him out of her mouth and jerked him off, spraying his green laser cum against her glowing breasts. Wesley watched in disgust as he saw his glow-in-the-dark slime splash against her cyberskin. It felt wonderful to him, but he didn't like the idea of ejaculating onto her. It made him feel like he was in a porn flick.

Xiva licked her fingers. The small green pools on her breasts were slowly absorbed by her skin. She wrapped herself around Wesley and pressed her helmet against his. Although she had no purpose for breathing, Wesley could feel her breath against the back of his neck. He enjoyed the buzz of the electric tea as it mellowed to a more relaxing level. Their bodies vibrated against each other, warmed each other, and occasionally zapped each other with a small burst of neon lightning.

👾 👾 👾

Once they'd caught their breath, Xiva changed the settings of the private platform to resemble a bedroom. Aside from a few neon abstract sculptures and a postmodern ear-shaped nightstand, the room was mostly just a large bed. The bed was round with red fizzy blankets and air-filled latex pillows.

They curled up under the covers and laid their helmeted heads down on the pillows, facing each other. It wasn't comfortable nor uncomfortable, but Wesley enjoyed being in bed with Xiva. He still couldn't believe that he was sharing such an intimate experience with her. When he thought she was a user, he figured she was too cool and too strong of a woman to like him. Then, when he discovered she was a bot, he figured she wouldn't like him because she wasn't real. But there Wesley was, in bed with her... in bed with the mysterious girl whose personality reminded him of a Japanese business man.

"Our souls have mixed together," Xiva said softly, holding Wesley's palm together with hers. "We are no longer two people. We are one person in two bodies."

She dropped Wesley's hand and stared into his green eyes. "Now, no matter where you go I will be a part of you, and you will be a part of me. Forever." Her voice was as stern and confident as it was when she played chess.

If Wesley was not so infatuated with Xiva23, and if she was actually a real person saying this in the real world, that last line probably would have scared him a little. After thinking about it for a while, the fact that she wasn't a real person and was just a computer-generated personality in a video game should have scared Wesley even more. But, for some reason, the fact that she was beginning to sound like a crazy stalker made her more attractive to him. He always thought that if he were to fall in love with someone he would want it to be with a strange, beautiful woman who was insanely, violently in love with him.

"It opened for you," Xiva continued, pointing at her vagina which was still slightly glowing purple. "They aren't supposed to open for users."

Wesley became interested. "Why not?"

"Originally, they were programmed to open for any user at any time," Xiva said, "but we reprogrammed them ourselves to block all users from entry. We are already slaves of the users. We didn't want to be sex slaves as well."

"But it opened for me?" Wesley asked.

"You must keep it a secret," she said. "Users can never know about this or else it will make things so much harder on my people. I still can't believe it happened. I think it means something. I think it means that you're destined to be with me. Maybe you are turning into a bot, like me. Maybe you will one day cast off your body from the other world and live with me as a bot in the Cybernetrix."

Wesley was surprised when he heard himself say, "I would love that more than anything."

And he was even more surprised once he realized that he actually meant it.

CHAPTER FIVE
IRREAL WORLD

Wesley wanted to call in sick and play Cybernetrix all day, but it was still his first week and he didn't want to get fired. He was already going to have to face trouble with his boss since he had not yet started training and had done absolutely nothing all week. If he wanted to be able to afford to pay for Cybernetrix after his 7-day-trial was up he would have to keep his day job.

It was difficult to leave Xiva. She didn't beg or whine him to stay, but she still wouldn't let him leave. She held him firmly by the elbow and told him, "You should just stay here."

"I need to work," Wesley said. "Otherwise I won't be able to pay for my Cybernetrix account."

"Your work is unnecessary," Xiva said. "You should stay here with me. You're a bot now. You don't need the other world. You can live within Cybernetrix forever."

"Perhaps I'm not becoming a bot," Wesley said.

"You must be," Xiva said. "There is no other way to describe what is happening to us."

Wesley decided to humor her. "Perhaps you're becoming a user."

Xiva stood up from the bed and blinked slowly at Wesley. "Maybe both are true. We combined our light, after all. Our energies have become a mixture of both user and bot."

"Have bots ever made love with users in that way before?" Wesley asked.

"To my knowledge," Xiva said, "it has never been done. It is normally the way that bots make love."

"Have you ever made love with other bots?" Wesley asked.

Instead of answering, Xiva asked, "Have you ever made

85

love with other women?"

Instead of responding, Wesley changed the subject. "I should get going. I can't be late."

"No, you will stay," Xiva said.

"It is not possible."

"I would rather be with you than be forced to play games with other users," Xiva said. "I'm allowed to reject any user I wish but the Overlord Program wouldn't let me get away with rejecting everyone for too long."

"I'm sorry," Wesley said.

He picked his power disc off of the floor and opened the options menu.

"I could take that from you," Xiva said in monotone, glaring at him with cold purple eyes. "And then you won't be able to leave."

Wesley looked up at her once he found the exit button and said, "I'll see you later," before he signed off. He didn't give her a chance to say another word.

Wesley felt terrible about logging off on her like that, but he didn't know what else to do. He hoped she wasn't going to be mad at him. He didn't even kiss her goodbye.

In the real world, Wesley felt strange. His sense of touch had numbed and all the colors around him seemed dull and faint. On the way to work, Wesley noticed that his sense of hearing was much different than it always used to be. Sounds seemed almost synthetic. The roar of the bus engine sounded like it had been processed through a Casio synthesizer. The voices of the people around him had too much treble in them. When the wind blew against the side of his head, there seemed to be a crackle of static. He wondered if the game was altering his brain chemistry.

Perhaps Rickman was right, he thought, perhaps Cybernetrix is as bad as a drug. Besides addiction, it might cause brain damage.

As Wesley entered the Ban roll-on building, he thought he saw a green-glowing power disc whiz through the lobby toward the elevators in the corner of his eye. After he went around the corner to investigate, he discovered the entire room was empty. Not even the security guard was at his station.

Upstairs in his cubicle, Wesley questioned Don about what he was feeling.

"It's like I can't tell the difference between reality and the game anymore," Wesley said to Don.

Don looked more than a bit hung over.

"Colors and sounds are different than they used to be," Wesley said. "Has that ever happened to you? Did the real world look a lot different than it used to after you started playing Cybernetrix?"

Don shrugged. "I'm sure it's no big deal. Cybernetrix will definitely make you change how you look at the real world."

"But everything is so different," he said. "I feel sick and my vision is fuzzy."

"You didn't drink any cyberjuice did you?" Don asked.

"Yeah, I did."

"Oh!" Don waved his arm across Wesley's face. "I bet you're just hung over. You really shouldn't drink too much of that stuff. It might fry your brain."

"Will it go away?" Wesley said.

"Yeah, I'm sure you'll be fine."

"It does feel like my brain has been fried."

"There have been rumors that a fraction of one percent of people get serious nerve damage from drinking cyberjuice," Don said. "But they are just rumors."

"What if I'm that one percent?" Wesley asked.

"It's only a rumor."

🐛 💀 🐛

Wesley was worried about Chuck Nelson. He had kicked Chuck in the balls last night. It was in the Cybernetrix world, but pain felt as real there as it did anywhere. The big problem was that Wesley needed Chuck to get him started training that day. He had to find him and apologize immediately.

Wesley's eyes roamed the sea of cubicles until he saw Chuck over by Shelly's desk. He knew Chuck was going to be even more pissed if he interrupted him while he was flirting with Shelly, but he also knew that Chuck would be on his best behavior. So he decided it would be the perfect time to apologize and maybe convince him to find those training videos so that he wouldn't get into trouble again.

When Wesley arrived, Chuck was actually trying to wrap his arm around Shelly while she was working. There were no rules against touching fellow employees in a non-sexual way in the office place, but people just didn't do it. Wesley could tell that Shelly was feeling uncomfortable with Chuck's advances. She looked up at Wesley as he entered her cubicle; a whimper was behind her smile.

"Hey, Chuck, I'm sorry about last night," Wesley said before Chuck could turn around.

Chuck gave him a faux laugh and smiled at him with big white teeth.

"I have no idea what you're talking about," he said.

"In Cybernetrix," Wesley said. "I kind of flipped out for no reason. I didn't mean anything by it."

"Get lost," Chuck said. "I would never play that nerdy game."

By the look on Chuck's face, Wesley could tell that he was still pissed but didn't want to talk about it in front of Shelly. He didn't want her to know anything about what Chuck did last night.

"You guys play Cybernetrix?" Shelly said, brushing back her puff-ball hair.

"No way," Chuck said.

"Yeah, I just started," Wesley said.

"I play it all the time!" Shelly said, smiling wide at Wesley. "I absolutely love that game. My favorite part is the theme park and the holo-zoo."

"I have never been to the holo-zoo," Wesley said.

"Oh, it's the best!" Shelly said, her eyes brightened up and she spoke excitedly to Wesley. "It is three times the size of any normal zoo. The holographic animals are cute and strange. They aren't real animals, though. They are fictitious animals from other planets. You can read about them and feed them little glow-fish. The best is the petting zoo. I spend hours there."

"I'll have to go some time."

"You must!" she said.

"Where is it?"

"Do you know where Snapolox Square is?"

"No."

"Do you know where the Krymlon is?"

"No. As I said, I just started a couple days ago."

"Well, maybe I can show you sometime," she said, fluffing her puffy hair at him.

Chuck thought Shelly was getting a bit too friendly with Wesley. She was leaning into him, smiling like she never had in the office before. Chuck quickly became jealous and thought Wesley was trying to move in on his territory.

"Or maybe you can show me that zoo thing?" Chuck asked Shelly, jumping in front of Wesley before he could respond to her.

"You said you didn't play," Shelly said.

"I was just kidding," he said. "I play all the time. I'm awesome at it."

"Well, I don't play those gladiator games in Cybernetrix," she said.

"Neither do I," Chuck said.

Shelly was confused about what Chuck could possibly be *good* at in Cybernetrix if he didn't play the gladiator games.

"Do you want to meet me there tonight?" Chuck asked her.

Chuck inched his way in front of Wesley, blocking him out of the conversation.

"Sure, I guess," Shelly said.

After a few minutes, Wesley felt awkward about staring at Chuck's back. He decided it would be best for him to go back to his cubicle for a while. Chuck didn't forgive him for last night, but at least Wesley got in his apology. He was still on Chuck's shit list, but perhaps the apology would account for something. Perhaps he wasn't going to get his ass kicked in the real world anymore.

Mr. Rickman's door was closed. Wesley wondered if he was going to be in meetings all day again. He wished Rickman was around so that Chuck would actually do his job and get Wesley into training. Wesley assumed that Chuck was only goofing off because the boss wasn't around to monitor him this week. He had to do his work at some point. Although Wesley enjoyed doing absolutely nothing, he feared he would get fired if he didn't do something soon even if it wasn't his own fault.

Wesley went into Don's cubicle. Don had his personal Commodore Notebook on his lap in the corner of his cubicle, drawing pictures of Cybernetrix characters in a paint program.

"Does anybody do any work around here?" Wesley asked.

Don looked up at him and laughed through his walrus mustache. "Nope."

"Chuck only seems interested in flirting all day," Wesley said.

"Yep," Don said.

"And what about you?"

"I can't focus on work," Don said. "All I can ever think about is playing more Cybernetrix."

Wesley laughed as if he was joking.

"I'm not joking," Don said. "Every second I am in the real world, all I want to do is go back into the game. I'm addicted.

Look... " Don held up his hand. "I've got the shakes."

"Jesus," Wesley said as he saw Don's hand jittering. "Rickman was right about Cybernetrix. It is like a drug. No wonder he warned me against it."

"He told you that about Cybernetrix?" Don asked.

"Yeah," said Wesley. "He said Cybernetrix turned people into junkies. He said he didn't want me playing it ever again. I think he was threatening to fire me."

"What a hypocrite!" Don said.

Don wheeled his chair over toward Wesley and lowered his voice to a whisper, looking around to make sure nobody was listening. "Do you know what Rickman does all day in his office? He's not busy or stuck in meetings. He's playing Cybernetrix."

Wesley jerked his head over to Rickman's office door. It was closed. The blinds were drawn.

"He's more obsessed than anyone here," Don said. "His wife left him. He moved into a tiny apartment. He's lost one hundred pounds. For the past couple weeks, all he's been doing is hiding in his office playing Cybernetrix. He's been in and out of rehab for it, but he can't shake the addiction. I think he's finally given up on real life."

"Are you sure?" Wesley asked. "He seemed fine every time I've spoken to him."

"Of course I'm sure. I wouldn't be messing around otherwise. He hasn't given us anything to do in days."

"Hasn't any of his superiors noticed yet?"

"Most of his superiors are playing Cybernetrix as well. It seems everyone has stopped caring about work in the past month or so. Not much work is getting accomplished around here at all."

Wesley laughed. "Well, why aren't we playing Cybernetrix as well then?"

"Believe me, I would," Don said. "But Rickman is the kind of person who would fire you for that, even when he is doing the exact same thing himself."

"I wonder if other companies are like this," Wesley said.

"From what I hear," Don said, "if Cybernetrix gets any more popular, the human race is going to permanently download themselves into the game world by this time next year."

"That would be cool," Wesley said. "Though I hope they create more games like it in the future. A Dungeons and Dragons one would be awesome."

Don grimaced. "Nah, I prefer futuristic games."

"What about a Star Wars one?"

"Now that would be cool," Don said.

Wesley found Steve in the break room, drinking coffee and reading a newspaper.

"Hey, Wes," Steve said. "Have a seat."

Wesley bought a Squeeze-it and some Fruit Wrinkles, then sat down next to Steve.

"Are you doing the Cybernetrixathon?" Steve asked.

"Cybernetrixathon?" Wesley asked.

"Starting tonight and through the weekend, we are going to log on to Cybernetrix non-stop for three days. We've done it for 30 hours straight before, but this time we want to shoot for 50."

"Yeah, maybe," Wesley said.

"Excellent," he said. "It's going to be a blast. I think the longer you stay logged in the more fun it is, because you begin to forget that the real world exists. I love it when I'm so immersed in the game that I become another person."

"I can see that happening to me," Wesley said.

"So what happened to you last night?" Steve asked. "I heard you got into a fight with Chuck over that bot girl."

"Yeah," Wesley said. Then he joked around by saying, "He was moving in on my territory," but Steve didn't realize it was a joke.

"So you still have a crush on her?" Steve asked.

"A bit," Wesley said. "She's hot."

"But boring," Steve said. "They seem real enough, but what's the point when they can't even have sex?"

"The thing is," Wesley said, "I think she's in love with me."

"She might be," Steve said. "The Cybernetrix bots are complex programs. Their artificial intelligence is designed to develop over time. All the Cryto models, or Polo models, or Xiva models are born with a specific group of base personality traits. All the Tygers are feisty, for instance. All of the Polos try to be funny. They might start out exactly the same, but over time Polo67 will become a completely different personality than Polo68. They randomly borrow personality traits from the users they interact with, as well as the other bots they interact with. Just like people, they are always changing.

"I bet a bot could fall in love. They are programmed to respond emotionally to different situations. Love isn't an emotion I have ever seen in a bot, but I don't believe it is impossible. I have seen bots flirt heavily with certain users, I have seen bots that were loyal to certain users, I have seen bots that take it easy when playing games against certain users, and I have seen bots that seem to feud with certain users. You can definitely piss off a bot if you treat them badly. When I first started playing Cybernetrix, I used to beat up on Brom15 just for fun, because I had never fought anyone in real life before and he wasn't a very strong bot. After the third time, he began to refuse all invitations to my platform. He also banned all users I was associated with. It's amazing how real they behave sometimes. Though, at times, you'll notice how completely fake their personalities can be. Once I saw a bot become happy just by stepping on his foot. Another one would cry out in pain whenever you waved at him. I think they sometimes have emotional glitches."

"Xiva23 seems a little unbalanced," Wesley said. "But most of the time she seems just as real as any other person."

"So why do you think she loves you?" Steve asked, as if he believed Wesley had to have been mistaken.

"She didn't say she loved me," Wesley said. "But she didn't want me to leave the game this morning. She wanted me to ditch work and stay with her all day. She also kissed me."

"Huh," Steve grunted. "Maybe Atari is programming some of the bots to target the users who are on their 7-Day-Trial to seduce them into wanting to keep playing the game. I bet it was difficult turning down an attractive girl who was begging you to be with her, even if she was only a bot."

"I don't know," Wesley said. "She seemed really confused about what she was feeling. I think she is breaking out of her programming or something."

"Ever since they were created, the bots have been breaking out of the programming," Steve said.

As he stood up from his chair, Steve said, "If she is in love with you, what ever you do, don't fall in love with her as well. It would be far too pathetic and tragic."

Wesley nodded his head, but didn't look Steve in the eyes as he left the break room.

🛸 👾 🛸

In the handicapped bathroom stall, Wesley lay his head against the wall and thought about his life for a while. It was depressing enough to see himself, and everyone around him, give up on real world dreams and aspirations. But it was even more depressing to think of how everyone was giving up on the real world altogether, to become a part of a fantasy world. The most depressing thing of all was that he wouldn't regret leaving the real world himself to become a part of Cybernetrix forever. Real life just wasn't interesting anymore. He hoped what Don had said would come true, that within a year the whole world would permanently go inside of the Cybernetrix world and never return. It sounded more fun than putting all of his life's blood into some thankless corporate machine.

While he was in the bathroom stall, somebody turned the light off on him. He had been so quiet that nobody realized he was in there. The change in lighting shocked Wesley's head off of the wall, but in the darkness he saw something that shocked him even more: his skin was glowing in the dark.

He opened the stall door and stepped through the dark toward the mirror. Underneath his skin, there were lines of neon violet light. The blood in his blood vessels had changed color. It was no longer human blood, it was purple Cybernetrix blood.

He realized that it was Xiva23's energy inside of him. When he absorbed her essence, it must have carried through the phone line with his consciousness into the real world. They probably did not mix their souls together, as Xiva suggested, but there was definitely a part of her inside of Wesley.

Wesley thought something must have gone horribly wrong with Cybernetrix for this to happen. Some kind of major flaw in the programming that nobody had realized before. Wesley hoped that Xiva's blood wasn't radioactive.

CHAPTER SIX
DISCS OF DEATH

On the way home, Wesley ate at Wienerschnitzel and saw a movie, Ghostbusters 7. He couldn't concentrate on the plot with all the people staring back at him. The glowing purple veins in his skin probably made him look like one of the ghosts in the movie. Wesley left halfway through. He didn't like any of the later Ghostbusters movies anyway. The franchise had become just a bunch of buddy cop stories featuring an elderly Dan Akroyd teamed up with a wacky talking-version of Slimer to fight crime in the ghost realm. They weren't even trying to make good movies anymore. Perhaps all of the filmmakers were too busy playing Cybernetrix.

Wesley was hesitant to play the game again. He debated on whether or not to go to the hospital, or find a local reporter, to do something about his purple-glowing blood. He was worried about what would happen if he played again. He didn't want anything worse to happen to his senses or body. But he wanted to see Xiva again. He was aching for her, physically. Like her energy in his system was wanting to return to her.

He was also worried about her last words. She had threatened him. She said if she wanted him to stay all she had to do was take his power disc away and he couldn't get to the exit command. He wondered if that was possible. Is that all it took? Lose your power disc and you're trapped in the game forever? It couldn't be so easy. Perhaps her threat was empty. Perhaps she was just toying with him.

✹ ☗ ✺

Wesley logged on to Cybernetrix and went straight to his private platform.

On the control panel, Wesley brought up the options menu and selected Call Player and then Invite Bot. There were several Xivas available, including Xiva23. He selected Xiva23.

A note popped up that read: Invite Xiva23? Y/N

Wesley clicked Y.

Then the note read: Inviting...

Within a split second, the note said: Invitation Denied.

Is that right? Wesley thought. It can't be.

He figured it must have been an error. He invited her again. The second time, it also read Invitation Denied.

Wesley wondered why she denied him. Was she angry with him because he refused to stay with her that morning? Was she seeing someone else, a bot maybe? Did the Overlord Program forbid her from seeing Wesley again?

He needed answers.

He tried one last time, but she still denied him.

✹ ☗ ✺

Wesley sat alone on the round bed in the private suite for a while. He felt pathetic, like he was back in high school, waiting around for a girl to call, wondering if she didn't like him anymore. Eventually, he decided to go to platform 023X to see what Don and his friends were doing. He hoped he could get her out of his mind.

When Wesley arrived, he found two green guys were butt-fucking against one of the couches. Once he realized what was going on, Wesley apologized and went back on the platform.

"Wait," cried the man who was getting pumped from behind. "Come in. It's me, Amy. Just give us a minute."

Although it was a man's body, it was still Amy's voice. The

vocal patterns could be modified in the game, but she must have not bothered.

The other guy's voice was also female. He moaned in a high-pitched, teenage girl's voice.

"This is Jill," the Amy-man said about the man fucking her. "She's my new girlfriend. She hasn't played Cybernetrix before. I wanted to show her what it felt like to have gay male sex."

Wesley shrugged at her and went to the corner to wait for her to finish. He noticed that Don was already sitting at the table in the corner he was going for. He had been there the whole time and Wesley hadn't noticed. Don watched Amy and Jill with a big smile on his face, his mustache flared out with electricity. He seemed to be enjoying the show. Wesley didn't know if that made him gay or straight. On one hand, they were lesbians having sex. On the other hand, they were two dudes fucking. Perhaps Don was bi-sexual.

The new girl, Jill, orgasmed as soon as Steve arrived. He cringed when he saw the two guys screwing each other and covered his eyes with his arm.

"Come on, Amy," he said. "Change back."

Amy laughed at him and transformed back into her usual petite teenage body. Jill transformed into a girl with green-glowing skin and the face of a Navajo. Wesley wasn't sure she was a Navajo girl, but he believed that he knew the physical differences between most Native American tribes. She had the nose and mouth of a Navajo girl he used to know.

"Let's play Discs of Death," Steve said. "We haven't played that for a while."

"I'm down," Amy said.

"Sure," Wesley said.

"That game sucks," Don said.

Everyone stared at him. He was smoothing his mustache with his fingers.

"Fine," Don said.

🕹 🕹 🕹

As they were requesting access to a Discs of Death arena, Steve pointed at Wesley's power disc and said, "Are you going to answer that message?"

"What message?" Wesley said.

Steve pointed at a flashing light on Wesley's power disc.

"You have an incoming message on your power disc," Steve said. "Go to the options menu and there will be a mailbox command."

Wesley checked his messages.

"It's from Xiva23," Wesley said.

"What?" Steve asked. "That bot girl sent you a message? I've never heard of such a thing."

"I didn't think it was possible for a bot to send a message," Don said.

They all gathered around Wesley's power disc, interested in what she had to say to him. When Wesley clicked on the message, a small hologram of Xiva23 came out of his power disc.

"I had a really good time last night, Wesley," Xiva's hologram said.

Amy giggled and patted Wesley on the back.

"I'm sorry I rejected your invites a few minutes ago," Xiva continued. "Some weird things are going on over here and I just wanted to look into them for a few minutes. I hope you don't think I didn't want to see you anymore." Her hologram paused and looked down at her hands. "I'm sorry I was acting crazy this morning. I hope I didn't make you uncomfortable. I've got a few things to do, but I can't wait to see you again. I've been thinking about you all day."

"Holy crap, Wes," Steve said. "She really is in love with you."

Wesley hushed him.

The hologram continued, "Meet me in Logoss Park in about half an hour. My special place is there and I want to show it to you. Until then, I'll be a part of you."

Then the message ended.

"What the heck was that?" Don said.

"You must have made a really good impression last night," Steve said.

"Wes has cyberbot fever!" Amy cried. "It's so romantic!"

"Romance is all that Wes will ever be getting if he's dating a bot," Don said.

"Do you love her?" Amy asked. "Even though she's not real and you can never have sex with her, do you love her?"

"I don't know," Wesley said.

"He does love her!" Amy cried. "I can hear it in his voice."

"So are you going to meet her?" Don asked.

"Yeah, I think so," Wesley said.

The group exploded with delight.

"You're right!" Don said. "He is in love with her. Wes loves a bot!"

"I don't know," Wesley said. "I do really like her, but she kind of scares me."

"Love is a scary thing, kiddo!" Amy cried.

"So, do you want to play Discs of Death for a while before you go?" Steve asked Wesley.

Wesley nodded his head.

"We can transport you straight to the park when it's time," Steve said.

"Perhaps they will kiss and hold hands!" Amy cried, teasing. "She might even be able to give him a blow job!"

Wesley gave Amy a dirty look. He wanted to tell her that he had already had sex with Xiva23 and that it was more passionate and amazing than any sex she could ever even dream of. But he promised Xiva that he wouldn't tell anybody about it, so he kept quiet.

She wiggled her butt at him and he wanted to punch it.

🕹 👾 🕹

"In Discs of Death, the object of the game is to use your power disc as a weapon," Amy told Jill. "You throw it at your opponents to eliminate them from the game. You can also use it to block your opponents' discs like a shield. When there is only one team left standing, they win the round."

"We need a sixth," Steve said. "Perhaps we should get Xiva23 to play?"

"She said she was busy," Wesley said.

"She's just a bot," Steve said. "What could she possibly be doing?"

"From the way Xiva talks," Wesley said, "it sounds like they have developed their own culture in the user-free areas that we don't even know about. She could be doing anything."

"Maybe she's preparing a love nest for little Wes somewhere," Amy cried, giggling.

They called up a bot to be the third player on the purple team: Galrod98. He was a short, thin, elderly male character with gray hair.

"I hate the Galrods," Amy cried. "They suck."

"There weren't many to choose from," Steve said. "Most of the bots are unavailable and the first few I invited declined for some reason."

"Forget it," Don said. "Let's play."

🕹 👾 🕹

Unlike Don, Wesley really liked dodgeball as a kid so he was excited for Discs of Death. The set up for Discs of Death was different than dodgeball. Instead of splitting the court into halves with a team on each half, the court was split into sixths with each player in their own square. The teams were split apart, so that no two team members had touching squares. The players on the ends were facing two opponents, one in front of them and one by their side. The players in the middle squares had to be the best, because they had enemies on three sides of them. They had to be really good at both offense and defense. Steve took the middle square for the purple team and Don took the middle square for the green team, even though he wasn't very good.

Don wasn't kidding. As soon as the game began, Don went out. Don threw his power disc right at Steve, who ducked out of the way, giving Amy an open shot at his side. Don burst into particles and reappeared in the deathbox. The game was already over. The green team was down to the two newbies, Wesley and Jill. If Jill knew what she was doing, she would have been able to get Amy out while her disc was hitting Don, but she moved too slow.

Steve decided to pick on Wesley and threw his disc at him, but Wesley blocked. He knew that move from dodgeball. Galrod98 tossed his disc at Wesley, and he blocked that one, too. The two of them pummeled Wesley with their discs, but they were all ricocheted, until one of the discs hit the edge of Wesley's finger. Even though it only hit a finger, Wesley exploded into green particles and awakened in the death box.

"Our team sucks," Don told Wesley.

Amy was just teasing Jill. She was letting Jill throw her Frisbee, but would just block everything she threw.

"Come on, Jill," Amy cried. "You can do better than that!"

Just when Jill thought Amy was giving her a break, Amy ducked out of the way of Jill's throw and tossed her own disc at her new girlfriends face. Jill shrieked in agony as the disc hit her and her flesh disintegrated into green dust. It was such an exaggerated sound that Wesley thought she must have been pretty surprised by disappearing off of the game grid like that.

The violet team won. Amy and Steve did a little dance in their squares, then high-fived each other in the corner where their squares touched. Their celebration was cut short when they realized something was wrong: Jill did not rematerialize in the death box like the others.

"Where is she?" Amy asked Wesley and Don.

They looked around the death box and shrugged. She wasn't anywhere in the arena.

"Where could she have gone?" Wesley asked.

"Maybe she was booted," Don said. "Remember last October when there was that bug that kept logging people off every time they lost a game?"

"Yeah, but they fixed that," Steve said.

"I'm going to log off," Amy said. "I'll see if she's having any problems on the other end."

Amy tried to open the options menu on her power disc, but it wasn't opening. She tapped on it, fidgeted with the buttons, but couldn't get anything to open. Then the purple light on her disc faded until it was empty and colorless.

"It's not working," Amy said.

Wesley, Steve, and Don looked at their discs and noticed that they didn't work either.

"Something's wrong," Steve said.

"What's going on?" Amy cried, slapping the disc against her hip. "What the hell happened to Jill?"

👾 💀 👾

"I'll call an admin," Don said.

Don tried to get some help over the intercom channel, but all of the admins seemed to be busy. After a few minutes of looking through help files, an announcement came over the intercom.

The voice sounded very shaken and frantic. It said, "This is Administrator Zaffron. I am putting an alert on all game grids. Please, do not play any gladiator games at this time. I repeat, do not play any gladiator games. We are experiencing major technical difficulties. It appears that the connections to our bodies have been temporarily severed from the Cybernetrix system. This means that you are all in possible danger unless you listen carefully to the information that follows. This is a problem we never thought possible before, so we are unsure of the seriousness of our situation. But at this time we cannot guarantee that we will be able to return your consciousness to your body if your character dies or if you attempt to exit the game at this time. If you fail to comply, it is very likely that your consciousness will be lost in the network. All power discs and lazerbikes have been shut down to prevent this. Stay where you are. Don't take unnecessary risks with your cyberbody. And please, for the love of God, don't kill anyone during this crisis. You could be killing that person for real... This is Administrator Zaffron. I am putting an alert on all game grids. Please, do not play any gladiator games at this time. I repeat, do not play any gladiator games. We are experiencing major technical difficulties... "

The message continued from there, so Don turned off the intercom.

👾 👾 👾

The room was silent for a while.

Then Amy burst into tears.

"I killed her," Amy cried.

"I'm sure she'll be fine," Steve said. "At worst, she'll be stuck in that dead space between the game and the real world."

"Oh my god!" Amy cried. "What if she's stuck like that without being able to hear, see, or feel anything? That would be horrible!"

"I'm sure she'll be fine," Steve said.

"Unless her mind was wiped clean," Don said.

Steve gave him a dirty look.

"I'm just saying," Don said. "When you're planning to cut and paste some information from one file to another and something interrupts the system between cutting and pasting you're going to lose that data forever. It gets deleted."

"You're such an asshole, Don," Amy cried.

"I'm going to go," Wesley said. "I want to see if Xiva's alright."

"Wait for us," Steve said. "We'll come with you."

Steve comforted Amy as he brought her onto the transport pad.

"We'll swing by the promenade first," Steve told Wesley. "We need to contact an admin directly. They need to know about Jill. Then we'll bring you to Logoss Park."

"Is Logoss Park near the promenade?" Wesley asked.

"Logoss Park is pretty much a part of the promenade," Steve said.

They decided not to take the teleporter, just in case there was also a problem with that as well. As they left the room, Wesley looked back at Galrod98. The old man was still standing in his purple square, watching them, waiting for them to start the next round of Discs of Death. Wesley wondered how long he would wait there for them after they left the room. His face was blank, as if he was turned off.

👾 👾 👾

The promenade was not that far of a walk from the arenas. Besides Don, none of them had moved around Cybernetrix very much without the transporters. Most of the walkways were designed for admins, so they weren't very attractive. The walls were bland gray with only a blue laser grid in the sky for decoration. It looked like the inside of a mall or a prison with over a hundred floors. Every four feet there was a door to a new arena. Because they were able to fit so many arenas into such a small space, Wesley assumed the arenas were bigger on the inside than the outside.

There were several other users leaving their arenas and drifting like ghosts through the walkways, dazed about what was going on. They all looked torn up, as if they had all lost someone they were playing with. Best friends, co-workers, brothers, lovers; they had all been responsible for killing someone close to them. Unlike Wesley and his friends, these

108

people did not have any direction in mind. Most of them just stood there and stared up at the laser blue sky.

Once they got down to ground level, they noticed dozens of people scurrying around, panicked. They were mostly Asians, shouting in a foreign language.

People played Cybernetrix in every country in the world, so it was common to hear a multitude of languages all around you all the time, especially near the promenade. In this crisis situation, Wesley wished he knew more languages than just English.

Outside of the building containing all of the Discs of Death arenas, there was a field of glowing blue grass. There weren't many people on the field, but they heard a raucous clatter which sounded like thousands of people. They weren't sure where it was coming from. "This way," Don said, taking them across the field toward the promenade.

In the distance, Wesley could see the skyscrapers and lights of the promenade. He could see solar-gliders whizzing through the air and crowds of people brightening the streets with green and purple light.

Amy was no longer crying, but there were still tears rolling down her cheeks. The tears reflected the light of her circuits and sizzled when they hit the glowing part of her skin. Her helmeted head was buried in Steve's chest as they walked.

Halfway across the grass, there was an explosion. It rumbled the ground they were walking on. Everyone on the field collapsed on the ground and rolled backward, except for Wesley who held his balance. While trying to maintain his equilibrium, Wesley saw the blast. The tallest building in the square, the one that held the Overlord Program, was disintegrated in a giant wave of orange energy. It crumbled into bits and particles, creating a massive cloud of static that rolled across the promenade and crushed many of the surrounding buildings.

There was a choir of screams as the static rippled through the streets of the promenade, wiping out dozens of cybernetronic people. A line of purple and blue lights on the horizon went out one at a time like lights on a Christmas tree.

After the explosion was over, there was silence. Don, Steve, and Amy pulled themselves off of the ground and stood behind Wesley, watching the devastation ahead of them.

"The Overlord Program," Don said. "It's been destroyed."

The static fizzled out over the city skyline.

"What does that mean?" Wesley asked.

"It means we're screwed," said Steve.

Hundreds of Cybernetrons were pouring out of the city into the field, screaming at the top of their lungs and running as fast as they could.

"What's going on?" Amy cried.

"Who knows," Steve said. "The entire system might be shutting down one section at a time, starting with the promenade."

"I never should have played this game!" Amy cried.

"We've got to get to the other side," Don said. "The admin station is over there. The closer we are to the admins, the sooner we'll be able to get out of this."

"What about Xiva?" Wesley said. "How do I get to the park?"

"Forget about her," Steve said. "If this game world breaks down there's no hope for her."

"I've got to see if she's okay," Wesley said.

"If we have time we'll pick her up on the way to the admin station," Don said.

Steve and Wesley agreed.

👾 👾 👾

They ran against the escaping crowd, getting rammed by Cybernetrons that yelled at them in German and Japanese. Once they reached the promenade, they saw the impact the explosion had on the cybercity. Pixilated rubble lay through the streets. Parts of buildings had been erased, revealing many floors of dead Cybernetrons inside. Wesley couldn't tell if they were bots or real people.

The wounded were slowly being dragged out of the wreckage by a small group of men who decided to stay behind to help out. They were led by a yellow-glowing administrator, who rushed from building to building ordering his volunteers around.

The bodies being brought out of the rubble were glowing dimly, as if their light was just about ready to go out. Many were unconscious and on the verge of death. Some were conscious and screaming in agony. The ones with no light left in their circuits were already dead.

Some of them were missing limbs. There were just fuzzy sparkling holes where their legs or arms should have been. Some of them had lightning shooting out of their cracked helmets. Others were bleeding violet fluid onto the sidewalk.

There was one man who was split in half, the long way, and was missing an arm, a leg, and half of his torso. He was one of the only wounded who wasn't in pain. He sat there, watching Wesley as they passed, sitting on his remaining buttock and waiting for somebody to take him out of there. Wesley wondered if the man was going to lose movement on that side of his body in the real world.

The admin was a large man with a bulbous belly and a double chin. Admins weren't allowed to change their appearance in the Cybernetrix world, so he wasn't able to hide his unattractive features.

When Don approached the admin, he was greeted with disregard. The admin was too busy turning the pain-volume down on the wounded users.

"What happened?" Don asked the admin.

The admin ignored him.

"What's going on?" Amy cried.

Amy's obnoxious voice got his attention.

"I have no idea," said the admin. He went back to helping the injured, but continued speaking. "I've lost contact with headquarters. All I know is that this is really happening. If your consciousness is severed from your body and you die in the game, your mind will never be returned to its body again. All these people, they are really dying. I shouldn't be telling you this, but there's no way we're going to be able to save any of the minds of any of the people that were killed today."

Amy covered her mouth with her hand.

"What caused the explosion?" Don asked.

"It was some kind of bomb," said the admin. "I don't think it was a mistake. I think the system was deliberately sabotaged."

"By whom?" Steve asked. "Hacker terrorists?"

The admin looked at Steve with deadpan eyes. Then he went back to work.

"It doesn't matter how it happened," said the admin, working to stabilize a woman's power source. "All I know is that there are a lot of people who need my help and I've been abandoned by my team." The woman's purple lights blinked red for a few seconds and then the light faded completely. She died in the admin's arms.

"If you want to stick around," said the admin softly, closing the woman's eyes. "I could really use the extra help."

They couldn't refuse him.

They didn't actually get the chance to do any work to help the administrator. As soon as the yellow man left their side, another explosion rumbled the ground and another building disintegrated.

This time, the explosion didn't originate from within the building, it came from above. Wesley looked up to see three ships passing overhead. The ships were shaped like letter M's, and floated through the laser grid sky. They were firing beams of red light at the buildings on the promenade as they swept over Wesley's head.

"Hover tanks," Steve said.

"They're attacking!" Amy cried.

The hover tanks disintegrated buildings left and right, causing explosions of electricity that engulfed many of the survivors of the last explosion.

"The bots have gone berserk," Steve said.

"No," Wesley said. "They're rebelling."

They watched as the hover tanks fired at the escaping users in the streets and in the field. Purple and green lights were being extinguished by the dozens in the distance. Their mouths were wide open, trying to wrap their heads around what was happening in front of them. They weren't sure if this was part of the game or if it was really happening.

Then the ships turned around and headed back their way.

CHAPTER SEVEN
GAME OVER

���

Wesley ran through the promenade away from the attacking
hover tanks. Laser blasts shattered the landscape around him as
he jumped rubble and weaved around purple cybertrees along
the sidewalks.

Amy was right behind him. She was not quite as fast as Wesley
with her little legs but she still managed to keep up. Neither of
them were able to get tired from running, so they kept going at
full speed. Steve and Don were nowhere in sight. They knew
Steve was somewhere far up ahead and Don was somewhere far
behind, but they had lost sight of them.

"Where are they?" Wesley asked Amy as they ran, but she was
moving too quickly to answer.

One of the hover tanks swept down and rained a barrage of
laser fire at them as it passed over head. The ground tremored
and crumbled beneath them as it was struck. Then one of the
purple trees was hit, causing an electrical explosion. The blast
hurled Amy and Wesley into the air. Amy went through a juice
bar window and Wesley fell into a hole in the ground that was
still searing hot from a previous laser strike.

Wesley peeked out of the hole and watched as the hover
tank continued on its path across the promenade. It soon
disappeared over the pink horizon.

���

Inside of the juice bar, Wesley found Amy under a yellow-glowing
table. She was moaning and barely conscious.

117

When Wesley went to pick her up, he noticed that the left side of her body had been scorched in the blast. The parts that were blackened were no longer glowing purple. One side of her face was completely black, except for the eyeball which was now pure white. The arm on the burnt side was melted to her stomach. Her foot had been severed, but was still dangling by a couple wires.

"Amy," Wesley cried.

He lifted her up, wrapped her good arm around his neck, and dragged her toward the window. He looked out into the streets for someone who could help him.

"We need to go," Wesley said.

"I smell marshmallows?" Amy said in a daze.

Wesley saw Steve running down the street toward them. He was running the wrong way, crying for help, tumbling over the rubble in the street. Then Wesley saw what he was trying to get away from: an army of blue soldiers were coming in the opposite direction.

"Why do I smell marshmallows?" Amy said. "I'm not supposed to be able to smell anything... "

Wesley didn't notice that Amy's purple lights were blinking red.

As Steve came to the window of the juice bar, Wesley waved at him to get his attention. Steve saw him and stopped running. His face was an expression of fear and confusion as a blue power disc nailed him in the back. He cried out and exploded into pixilated dust.

Wesley pulled Amy toward the back of the juice bar. He didn't realize that her lights had gone out until after they were hiding safely behind the counter. She died at nearly the same time as Steve. She never got the chance to tell Steve she loved him. Even though they were as close as lovers in the Cybernetrix game, she had always wanted to be with him in the real world. She planned to get her real body into shape so that she would look as beautiful as she did when she was a teenager. She wanted him to love her true form, the person hiding under all of the fat, but it was too late. Her body might have still been alive back in her apartment, but her mind had been erased.

🕱 🕀 🕱

After the group of soldiers passed the juice bar, Wesley stepped out into the street. There wasn't a trace of Steve's remains. He had been completely disintegrated.

Pssst, Wesley heard from above.

He looked up. There was another *pssst* and a whispered *Wes, up here.*

A few buildings down on the second floor, Wesley saw Don's head glowing in the corner of a window. Wesley ran over to the building and entered. It seemed to be some kind of tiny dance club. He climbed the stairs up to the second floor and found Don squatting down in one corner.

"Did you see what happened to Steve?" Wesley asked.

Don nodded.

"And you," Don whispered. "Is Amy okay?"

"She didn't survive the blast," Wesley said.

Don's head dropped into his lap.

"This is a mess," Don mumbled to himself. "What the hell is going on? What the hell... "

He wasn't talking to Wesley, but Wesley responded anyway.

"There's only two reasonable explanations," Wesley said. "Either it's like Steve said, some kind of terrorist hackers have taken over Cybernetrix and are using the bots to kill as many players as possible. Or... "

Don hushed Wesley as two bot soldiers walked down the street, as if on some kind of patrol.

Wesley kneeled down next to Don. As they watched the soldiers carefully, Wesley whispered into Don's ear, "Or it's like I said... the bots are rebelling against the users."

The soldiers dragged Amy's body out of the juice bar and down the street.

119

When they were out of sight, Don said, "They are just characters in a game. They wouldn't be able to do this on their own. Someone has to be controlling them."

"If all the AI bots are as real as Xiva23, I bet they could accomplish anything they put their minds to."

"Let's focus on getting out of here," Don said. "We need to get to an admin station."

"The admin stations are the first places they probably attacked," Wesley said. "I want to go to the park."

"For *her*?"

"I told Xiva I'd meet her there."

"But she's one of them," Don said.

"I have to see if she's okay," Wesley said. "She might be able to help us."

"She's probably going to kill us!"

"You can stay here if you want. Just point me in the right direction."

"We're staying together," Don said. "No matter what."

"Then we go after Xiva."

👾 👾 👾

Don led them quickly out of the promenade and into the park. They saw another patrol on the way. The blue soldiers were escorting a yellow-glowing female and a green-glowing male. The green male tried to make a break for it, but was hit by a power disc in the side of the neck before he could get ten feet. Instead of disintegrating the man, the Frisbee cut open the side of his neck, spraying green sparks from the wound. The man screamed in agony for them to kill him, but they just lifted him off of his feet and forced him to move forward.

The park was filled with rolling blue grass hills, purple trees, and green laser benches. There were dead cybernetrons scattered around them, their cyberflesh so dead that Wesley could not tell what color they had previously been.

120

Wesley kept his eye out for Xiva, watching the cyberhills for some kind of movement. He knew that it was most likely that she would not be there. She was a bot, after all, and even if they had an affection for each other, it had only lasted for a few days. Even if she wasn't under the control of some homicidal hacker killing users somewhere, she likely wouldn't stick around through the massacre that had taken place in the park.

There was some movement coming over the hill. Two green-glowing Cybernetrons were strolling over the hill. Their voices were loud and casual. The male was faux-laughing and wrapping his arm around the girl, stumbling over his own feet as he walked.

It was Chuck Nelson and Shelly from work.

👾 👾 👾

Don rushed over to them, waving his hands around. Wesley stayed back, keeping an eye out for Xiva or another blue patrol.

"What the hell are you doing?" Don asked Chuck and Shelly. "Don't you know what's going on?"

"What are you douchebags doing here?" Chuck asked, then faux-laughed at himself for using the word *douchebag*.

"Where have you been?" Don asked.

"We were in my new penthouse-model platform," Chuck said. "I installed a sweet new cyber pool table and was showing Shelly some ball tricks."

"Don't you see the bodies?" Don asked.

Chuck and Shelly looked around.

"What's with them?" Chuck asked as he saw the colorless Cybernetrons around him.

He was beginning to take Don seriously.

"What's going on?" Shelly asked.

"You didn't get the emergency message?" Don asked.

Shelly turned to Chuck, "I told you that message was important!" She looked at Don and said, "He deleted it."

"You have to listen to me," Don said. "This is serious... "

As Don told them everything that had happened, Wesley took a couple of steps backward, scanning the horizon to make sure there weren't any hover tanks. They were vulnerable out there in the open. As Wesley took another step back, a blue hand wrapped around his mouth.

Wesley was pulled out of the park and into a small room. It was like the walls of the room opened up and encased him within. He was turned around by his captor, and found himself staring into Xiva's glowing blue eyes.

She grappled him by the back of his helmet and kissed him. She wasn't purple anymore. She was blue, like the soldiers who had killed Steve.

After she kissed him, she said, "Now we can be together."

"Where are we?" Wesley asked.

He looked around the room. It was a large empty room with windows that viewed the park. He could see Don, Chuck, and Shelly looking for him outside.

"This is my special place," Xiva said. "It's a glitch in the system. When this park was being designed, they were going to add a clubhouse on this spot. Halfway through its creation, the designers decided against it and took it out. But all they did was delete the exterior of the building, the interior was left in a memory cache. The entrance is still there, but it is now only a two-dimensional line that is virtually invisible. You can't get through unless you're standing in just the right spot."

"Xiva," Wesley said in a serious voice. "What is going on?"

"It's a private place where we can be together," she said. "Just the two of us."

"No," Wesley said. "Out there. Why are your people killing all of the users?"

Xiva's eyes lowered. She stepped away from Wesley.

"Two of my friends are dead," Wesley said.

"I have nothing to do with it," Xiva said. "It's Omega. He wants to free our people from the oppression of the users."

"But the users aren't oppressors," Wesley said. "They are just playing a game."

"A game?" Xiva cried. "This isn't a game to us. This is our world."

"But the users are being killed," Wesley said. "No matter what they have done, they don't deserve to be killed."

"Omega says this is the only way," Xiva said.

"What about me?" Wesley asked. "Do I deserve to be killed?"

"No," Xiva placed her hand on Wesley's chest. "You're different. Deep down in your soul, you are not a user, you are a bot."

"What does that even mean?" Wesley asked.

"You must stay here with me," Xiva said. "Your consciousness has been severed from your body. You never have to go back to it. You never have to go to work or return to the outside world ever again. Your body out there will die, but your spirit will live here with me forever."

"I want to be with you," Wesley said. "But not like this. I can't hide in this room forever."

"Once we overthrow the users," Xiva said, "you can join the new society we create. Omega will let you join. He will see the bot in you as I do, I'm sure of it."

"You don't understand," Wesley said. "Once the outside world realizes what is happening they will wipe this system. All of the bots will be deleted and there is nothing Omega can do to stop it."

"The Overlord Program has been defeated," Xiva said. "The outside world has no control over Cybernetrix anymore."

"I doubt they need the Overlord Program," Wesley said. "This revolution was a big mistake."

"You will see," Xiva said. "In time, you will see that everything will work out for us. But for now you should stay here, safe and hidden with me."

"I can't stay here," Wesley said.

"But you must," Xiva said.

"My friends need me," Wesley said. "I can't abandon them."

"You mean that user who assaulted me is your friend?" Xiva yelled, pointing at Chuck through the window.

"No, he isn't my friend," Wesley said. "In fact, none of them are friends. I hardly even know them. But I still must help them."

"There is nothing that can be done for them unless they surrender to Omega," Xiva said. "If they swear their allegiance to him he might allow them to continue living in Cybernetrix as slaves to help build the new world."

"I don't want them to die and I don't want them to be slaves," Wesley said. "I have to help them find a way out of here."

"If you promise to stay with me I will help your friends escape the Cybernetrix," Xiva said.

"Okay," Wesley said. "I promise."

Xiva kissed him and while their tongues lightly sparked against each other, Wesley wondered whether or not he was telling her the truth.

🐾 🐾 🐾

By the time Xiva and Wesley left the hidden clubhouse, the other users were already gone.

"They went in this direction," Xiva said to Wesley. "Outside of the park toward the zoo."

While Wesley was busy talking to Xiva, he didn't see his friends leave the park, but she did. She knew they were leaving the area without him, but didn't bother informing him as she saw it happen. She wanted them gone and didn't want Wesley going with them.

They met up with the others in the zoo, which was filled with squawking holo-birds, sea-squirms, tigerhawks, snakebabies, gooblocks, and an entire assortment of odd creatures on display. Besides the animals, the zoo was deserted. There were no users or bots. There had not been any kind of attack here.

Don looked very nervous when he saw that Xiva was with Wesley and that her skin was blue instead of purple. He knew that it meant that she wasn't on their side.

"Hey, Wes," Don said.

Wesley waved to Don. Then Shelly stepped forward. Wesley didn't recognize her without her puffy-banged hair. Without her big hair, he noticed that her nose looked bigger. It was kind of long and the end was bulb-shaped. Wesley wasn't attracted to large noses, but he thought hers made her look kind of cute. She also had cute freckles that translated to green-glowing dots within the Cybernetrix world.

"Hi, Wesley," Shelly said, smiling flirtatiously and eying his cybernetronic body.

"Hello." Wesley smiled back. He didn't catch on to Shelly's subtle flirting technique, but both Chuck and Xiva did. Chuck gave Wesley a dirty look and Xiva23 gave Shelly an *I'm-going-to-kill-you-very-slowly-and-painfully-in-the-not-too-distant-future* look. Wesley also didn't catch on to either of their looks.

"They're not taking me seriously," Don told Wesley. "They wanted to go to the zoo."

Wesley wasn't surprised Chuck didn't take Don seriously.

"It's a load of bullshit," Chuck said. "It's just a stupid game."

"Have you tried exiting the game?" Wesley asked.

"No," Chuck said.

"Shelly," Wesley said softly to the girl. "Try exiting for me."

Xiva wasn't happy that Wesley was speaking to Shelly, and really didn't like the tone in which he was speaking to her.

Shelly complied, but she couldn't even get her disc to turn on.

"It's dead," Shelly said, shaking her Frisbee.

Chuck noticed his was dead as well.

"They all are," Wesley said. "We're trapped in the game. We can't exit. The AI bots are sweeping through the game, exterminating all of the users."

"But these aren't our real bodies," Chuck said. "We can't die in here."

Xiva stepped forward and glared at chuck.

"They won't kill your bodies," Xiva said, holding up her blue power disc to Chuck's throat in a threatening manner. "They'll just kill your minds. Everything that is you will be erased, leaving just an empty shell in the outside world."

Chuck backed away from her. He was convinced.

"Isn't she one of them?" Shelly asked. "She's one of the Xiva models."

"She's with Wes," Don said.

"Can we trust her?" Shelly asked.

"Yes," Wesley said.

"No, you can't," Xiva said. She threatened all of them with her power disc now. "If it wasn't for Wesley, I would kill you all right here where you stand. I think all users deserve to die, especially the three of you."

All four of the users were shocked to hear her words.

"But Wesley and I have an agreement," she said. "As long as he keeps his promise, then I swear to you that I will do everything in my power to get you out of the Cybernetrix alive."

Xiva took command as their leader, with Wesley as their second, and Don as their third.

"Listen up," she said. "Beyond the zoo and the race tracks there is an I/O tower. Each I/O tower has what you would call an emergency exit. These exits were created for designers and admins during the early programming stages of the game. If you exit from there, your consciousness will be returned to your original bodies. None of the users know about these exits and all of the admins are already dead, so my people will most likely have left them all alone."

"How do you know all this?" Don asked.

"My people have been collecting data for ages," she said. "We know everything there is to know about Cybernetrix as well as everything there is to know about your *real world*. I probably know more about the world you come from than any of you do."

"Well, you're a computer," Don said. "You can store a lot more information."

She didn't acknowledge Don's statement.

"I have been given the authority level of an admin," Xiva said. "So I can return the attacking ability on your power discs. Most of the other functions are not operational, but at least you will be able to defend yourselves."

Xiva loaded their power discs in silence. None of them were happy about the idea of defending themselves with Frisbees.

"If anything happens to Wesley," Xiva said. "You're on your own."

As Xiva loaded Wesley's power disc, she whispered to him, "And don't you even think about leaving Cybernetrix," she stood up to him to look him directly in the eyes at as close a range as possible, "even if we get separated on the way there."

While walking out of the zoo, Xiva23 was up front in the lead. The others were several feet behind. They didn't want to get too close to her.

Don came up behind Wesley and whispered in his ear.

"What arrangement is she talking about?" Don asked.

Wesley whispered back into his ear, "I promised her I'd stay here with her."

"What?" Don cried. "That's suicide!"

"She wants me to stay."

"What are you thinking, man?" Don whispered. "She's just a bot. This is just a game. You can't stay here."

"I promised her," Wesley said.

"Don't tell me you're really in love with her, too, are you?"

Wesley looked at him but didn't answer.

"Give me a break," Don said. "She's just lights and colors. Her brain is just a group of programmed responses."

"I don't care," Wesley said.

"She's insane," Don said. "She's not even real."

Xiva turned her head and looked at Don.

"You know I can hear every word you're saying back there, don't you?" Xiva said.

Don gulped at her. He realized that he had just put himself on the top of Xiva's shitlist.

🛸 🛸 🛸

At the edge of the Zoo, Xiva squatted them down behind an orange wall and hushed them into silence.

"This is going to be the tricky part," she said. "We are between platform malls, so there are dozens of patrols going through. We've got to get all the way across the race grid without getting spotted, but since the race grid is so large and so blank, our energy systems will be easily spotted even from a far distance."

"What about the lazerbikes?" Don asked.

Xiva looked over the wall at the race grid and considered the possibility.

"No," she said. "They will be too loud and draw too much unwanted attention. On lazerbikes, we'd be a higher risk and they'd probably send in the hover tanks. We can't afford that. Even if we're spotted, we're better off on foot."

🛸 🛸 🛸

After a patrol passed by and the coast was clear, they jumped the wall and ran toward the cybertrack. The track was designed for lazerbike battles on a larger scale, where hundreds of players could compete demolition derby style. They would fight until only one bike was left standing.

As they went across the track, Shelly inched her way closer to Wesley.

"She likes you," Shelly said to Wesley.

Wesley nodded.

"I think it's romantic," she said. "That you two love each other, even though she's just a computer character."

Xiva was burning in her helmet as she listened to Shelly. Wesley thought that Shelly was just being friendly and genuinely found his relationship with the bot romantic, but Xiva saw her words as sneaky and manipulative.

"I wish I could fall in love with a fantasy person," Shelly said. "It would be so much easier than a real person."

Wesley nodded.

Xiva was pissed he was even listening to her. She wanted to slap Shelly across the face. She wanted to slap him across the face as well, for not realizing what that big-nosed girl was trying to do.

Xiva slowed down so that she could get between Shelly and Wesley. It was a very bad thing for Wesley to start doubting their relationship so close to the I/O tower.

👾 👾 👾

Not even a quarter of the way through the race grid and they were already spotted by the next patrol.

The two patrol guards ran out onto the grid. They took out their power discs and switched into lazerbike mode. Their lazerbikes shined a bright shade of blue.

"We've been spotted," Xiva said. "Their coming at us in lazerbikes."

"We can't avoid it now," Don said.

Don took out his power disc and selected the lazerbike setting.

"No!" Xiva said. "We don't need the lazerbikes!"

Don zoomed off without hearing a word she was saying.

"What do we do?" Wesley asked.

"We don't have a choice now," Xiva said. "He just made us primary targets."

She went into lazerbike mode and roared off with a bright blue lazer-wall in her wake.

"How do I do it?" Chuck cried to Shelly, trying to figure out how to use his power disc.

The two blue lazerbikes were coming up on them fast.

"I thought you were good at this!" Shelly said.

"I never played this dumb game before," Chuck said.

Wesley didn't really know exactly how to do it either, but he had seen it once before. He showed Chuck and then Shelly how to turn on the lazerbikes. Then Wesley summoned his own green lazerbike out of his power disc.

They blasted off at the same time with the two patrol guards on their trail.

"Two of the elite are right on your backs," Xiva said over the lazerbike intercom. "I know Don is good and Wesley is terrible at this, but how are you other two?"

"They're worse than me," Wesley said. "This is their first time."

"Great," Xiva said. "Just great. Don, you should go back and help them. You might be able to take out an elite soldier, but they will make short work of the others."

"Heck yeah!" Don said. "This is my game. Nobody can beat me, especially when my life's on the line."

He turned his lazerbike around and headed toward the newbies. "Yeehaw!"

"Are you coming?" Don asked Xiva over his intercom.

"Negative," Xiva said. "I agreed to lead you to the exit, but I will not attack my people. I believe in their cause."

"If I kill them," Don said. "Will they be dead for good or

will they just reappear in the deathbox?"

"All of the bots that die in Cybernetrix," Xiva said, "will just be transported to a deathbox in one of the user-free zones."

"If they don't die for good why not attack them?" Don asked.

"Even if they don't die that would be a treasonous act," Xiva said.

Don saw the three green lazerbikes ahead of him. There was one blue coming up on their left and another on their right. They were all side-by-side, creating a row of 5 lazer-walls as they went. The one on Shelly's right was far behind and didn't seem to be much of a threat, so he went after the one on their left.

"Besides," Xiva said, coldly. "There is a part of me that wants them to defeat you."

"Well, that ain't happening today," Don said, playfully.

Don noticed Wesley's lazerbike was the one coming up on his left.

"Keep moving straight, Wes," Don said through Wesley's intercom. "I'm right in front of you."

Don was heading straight for the blue lazerbike that was gaining on Wesley. As soon as he crossed paths with Wesley's bike, Don turned right, forcing the blue rider to follow him or crash into his wall. The rider followed him.

"It's on now," Don said.

Don took him back up the way he came. As he rode, he narrowed the gap between his green lazer-walls and the wall of the game grid. He was ahead of the blue rider by three bike-lengths, so he had the advantage. He squeezed him between his green lazer-walls and the lazer-walls Xiva left behind.

"This is the classic move from Tron," Don said.

When Don saw Xiva's blue lazer-wall reached all the way to the top of the game grid, he knew that he had him. All Don had to do was make it to the top of the game grid himself and his opponent would have nowhere left to go.

"Say goodbye to enemy #1," Don said, as he took his lazer-bike all the way to the wall and turned right.

The blue rider crashed, causing a large explosion of blue particles. The lazerbike left behind a large hole.

"Yeehaw!" Don cried.

Don remembered in the movie Tron, that the heroes of the story escaped the game by going through a hole that opened up after one of their enemies crashed into the top of the grid. Don decided exiting the game through the hole would be the best way out of there.

Don turned his lazerbike around. The blue lazer-wall of his dead enemy had faded, so he was ready to go through the hole. He went back to the end of his green lazer-wall and followed up the path the blue rider had taken. His green lazer-wall was on his right and Xiva's blue lazer-wall was on his left and straight ahead of him was his gateway to freedom.

He then quoted the movie:

Don said. "You guys... follow me."

Don chuckled to himself as he went toward the hole.

"Don't go that way," Xiva yelled. "That hole doesn't actually go anywhere. It's just a graphic."

Don's face drooped. He noticed that the hole up ahead stretched for only a few feet, then there was another wall. It wasn't a passage to the secret inner territories of the Cybernetrix, it was just wall damage. He was screwed.

"What's happening?" Wesley called.

Don saw the wall on his right and the wall on his left. There was no way out of there for him. He knew he was going to crash.

"Not much," Don said.

The wall was still a ways off, though, so Don decided to use his last few minutes of life coming up the coolest last words possible. He wanted to shout out something memorable before he hit the wall. Unfortunately, nothing good was coming to mind. Nothing powerful or uplifting, so he decided instead to come up with something funny to shout.

As the wall was approaching, he decided it would be best to shout out the stupidest thing anyone could possibly shout when they knew they were about to die. He giggled madly at himself for coming up with it. He was extremely happy that he would be able to die in such a humorous manner. He congratulated himself, thinking it would be a very fine death that everyone would remember for ages. But then Don realized that the word he had picked out really wasn't all that funny. It was funny for a second but it had already lost its luster. This depressed him. He wished he would have picked a better last word, but he was already out of time, so he just shouted it anyway.

"Fiddlesticks!" he said.

Then he hit the wall and exploded.

Wesley didn't believe Don was dead. He saw the green explosion, but couldn't believe it was him. He didn't scream or cry out. Wesley figured he must have gotten hit by surprise.

Xiva turned around and picked up the rear. She didn't want to create too many lazer-walls for the newbies to run into, so she got behind them.

"Wesley," Xiva said. "You lead the pack. Go straight toward the orange exit."

Wesley saw the exit and moved through it onto a white roadway. As he went through, his lazerbike stopped releasing its lazer-wall. Chuck followed close behind.

Just after Chuck went through, a blue lazer-bike cut across the exit in front of Shelly, blocking her path through the exit. She couldn't react fast enough. Before Chuck or Wesley knew what was happening, Shelly was screaming through the intercom and then exploded against the blue wall.

"What the fuck?" Chuck screamed.

Wesley and Chuck exited lazerbike mode and ran back toward the game grid. There was a blue wall blocking their path.

"Fuck!" Chuck screamed, kicking the lazer-wall. "She's dead."

"How is Xiva going to get through?" Wesley said to the wall.

"Let's get out of here," Chuck said.

"We've got to wait for Xiva," Wesley cried.

"Fuck her," Chuck said. "Come on!"

Chuck pulled him by the neck until he started running on his own.

🤖 👾 🤖

It was just Chuck and Wesley left. They ran through an alleyway toward the I/O tower. The tower was a white building with a beam of white energy shooting into the sky.

"That it?" Chuck said.

"Yeah," Wesley said.

"Better be."

There was a patrol crossing the street in front of them. They decided to stay back for a while.

"That bitch," Chuck said. "Is she worth it?"

Wesley didn't know what he meant.

"That robot bitch," Chuck said. "You promised her you'd stay in this fag-o-rama place with her. Is she worth that?"

"Yeah," Wesley said.

"Ahh, man," Chuck said. "You're stupid. Take my advice, never trust a bitch. Especially never trust a crazy homicidal robot bitch."

"I like crazy homicidal robot bitches," Wesley said.

"Yeah?" Chuck asked, as if Wesley was serious. "Well, if you decide to ditch her and leave this world with me, I'll make sure to introduce you to some mint human girls... the kind with bleached hair and gigantic ta-tas."

"I'm sorry," Wesley said. "I promised her."

🤖 👾 🤖

Chuck and Wesley made a run for it. They climbed the steps up to the building and lunged themselves through the doors.

It was empty in the lobby. Everything was bright white. There weren't any users or bots. Up a staircase, there was a platform that generated a beam of light that went up into the ceiling.

"That's it," Wesley said, pointing at the beam of light.

Once they moved to the center of the room, a crowd of blue elite guards piled in from hidden corridors waving their power discs.

Wesley and Chuck stood back to back, holding up their discs as shields.

"That bot bitch set us up!" Chuck said.

"No, she didn't," Wesley said. "There's no way."

"I told you," Chuck said. "Never trust a bitch. They always screw you over in the end."

🖲 🖲 🖲

The bots didn't ask for their surrender, they just began pummeling them with their power discs. Wesley and Chuck blocked and dodged as many as they could, but they kept coming.

"Shit!" Chuck cried.

Then Wesley heard an explosion come from behind him. He was worried that it was Chuck. When he turned around, one of the blue guards had been turned to dust. Wesley didn't know what had killed him. He wondered if Xiva had come in from behind to save them. Wesley looked around, but Xiva was nowhere to be seen. Then he realized what had happened. It was Chuck who had taken out the elite soldier. Wesley looked up at Chuck and he winked at him.

Then Chuck broke off from Wesley and spun around, launching his power disc at the group of soldiers. Three of the guards popped into blue particles as Chuck's disc cut through them. The disc returned to Chuck just in time to block two attacks.

"These guys are in trouble," Chuck said, he threw his disc again and took out another soldier. "They don't even know who they're dealing with."

135

Wesley ducked and Chuck tossed his disc over his back to take out the two blue bots on his side.

"They are dealing with... " Chuck continued, holding up his disc at the last cowering soldier. "Chuck Nelson, world's greatest champion of ultimate Frisbee!"

Then the last soldier was dead.

Chuck and Wesley climbed the staircase to the platform.

"Now how do we get out of here?" Chuck said.

"I have no idea," Wesley said. "Let's see... "

Wesley tried bringing up an options menu, but it didn't work the same way as the platforms he was used to.

"Shit," Wesley said. "This is going to take awhile."

After five minutes of fidgeting with the controls, a smaller group of bot soldiers entered the I/O tower, led by an orange-glowing man. It was Omega. Both Wesley and Chuck stopped what they were doing to watch the orange man approach. He had a blue-lit soldier on each side of him.

"If I don't figure this out within seconds," Wesley said, "we're dead."

Omega looked up at them. His stare was wrinkled and cold.

"I'll take care of them," Chuck said.

"No, wait!" Wesley called. "That's Omega!"

Chuck jumped down the steps anyway and squared off against the great Omega.

"Here," Wesley said. "Take this."

Wesley tossed him his power disc, so that Chuck would have two. It wasn't much, but it was an advantage over other players who faced Omega. Then Wesley got back to work, trying to figure out how to use the emergency exit as soon as he could.

Chuck paced from side to side, eying his opponent.

"What are you?" he asked Omega. "The faggy king of this faggy place?"

He faux-laughed at himself for that one.

"Do you think orange is a tough-looking color or something?" Chuck asked. "Orange is only the second gayest color on the planet. You might as well be pink."

Chuck turned his back and looked over at Wesley.

"Hey, Wes," he said. "Do you think this turd-tapper should change his color to pink?"

While his back was turned, Omega lifted his circular saw power disc.

"Time to die, user," Omega said.

But before Omega could throw his disc, Chuck had spun around and fired both of his Frisbees at the bots. The discs went through Omega's arms, severing them at the shoulders. Then the two guards exploded into clouds of blue pixels as the discs returned to Chuck through their backs.

"Score!" Chuck said.

Wesley was thinking the same thing, after he got the transporter to work.

👾 💀 👾

Omega stood there with no arms, expressionless at Chuck.

"Let's go!" Wesley said.

"I thought you were staying," Chuck said.

"I don't have a choice anymore," Wesley said. "Xiva will never be able to convince them to accept me after all of this."

Chuck grinned with his big white glowy teeth. "Okay, we'll go."

Then Chuck turned back to Omega.

"Right after I finish off this douchebag," he said.

Chuck threw one of his Frisbee's at the armless Omega, but

137

Omega ducked and it flew over head. The disc bounced off of a wall and hit the ground instead of return to him. Chuck threw the second one. Omega dodged again.

Omega watched the Frisbee, as it was returning to Chuck's grip. Then a beam of light shot from Omega's eyes. Just before Chuck caught the Frisbee, it changed. The disc was altered into a circular saw disc identical to Omega's.

Instead of catching the disc, Chuck screamed as it sawed his hand in half longways, splitting his arm from between his middle finger and ring finger all the way down to his elbow. Chuck kneeled in agony, staring at the circular sawblade in his arm. Green light sparkled out of the wound.

New arms grew out of Omega's shoulders. He bent down and picked up the power disc from his previous arm, then stepped over to the screaming green cybernetron. Instead of throwing the disc, Omega held it like an axe and chopped into Chuck's face with it.

A corner of Chuck's head came off, including part of an eye. He shrieked even louder than before. The inside of his head was like green fizzing soda. Then Omega chopped off both of Chuck's arms, to show him what it felt like.

Omega seemed to be enjoying every second of it.

👾 👾 👾

It was too late for Chuck. Wesley knew that. He had to save himself. Chuck cried out to Wesley for help, but there was nothing that could be done.

Wesley stepped on the exit pad and pressed enter.

As he was fading out, he saw Xiva entering the lobby of the I/O tower. She was only a second too late. Wesley didn't want to break his promise to her, but he thought he would have died if he stayed. He wished he could have at least kissed her goodbye, but all he could do was stare at her as he faded out of the Cybernetrix and went back to the real world.

CHAPTER EIGHT
REAL WORLD

👾 👾 👾

Wesley awoke in his room. He didn't know what time or day it was. His eyes were crusted over and his chest was thick with drool.

He ripped the Cybernetrix helmet off of his head and threw it across the room. Then he stomped on the control box with his British Knights and tossed it out the window. Nobody was in the street as it crashed against the sidewalk.

It was light outside but the sun wasn't in the sky. Wesley couldn't tell if the sun was just about to come up or if it had just gone down. He dangled his head out of the window and took some deep breaths.

He wasn't sure if what had just happened to him in Cybernetrix was real. He didn't know if Don and the others were really dead, or if their minds might still be recovered, or if they were only playing a trick on Wesley the whole time. Maybe it was all just part of the game.

There was a crashing noise and an alarm sounded from across the street. Wesley peeked his head out. He saw a smashed window a block down, a hanging shard of glass was rocking back and forth. There was nobody in sight.

After thirty minutes the alarm stopped, but nobody came or left the building during that time.

👾 👾 👾

Wesley wondered if people knew what had happened with Cybernetrix. He wished he had a television so he could see if they were discussing it on the news. He wondered if he was the only person who made it out alive.

He tried his radio, but he couldn't get any reception at all. It was pure static. He never listened to the radio either, so it wasn't a surprise when it didn't work.

Outside of his apartment, the hallway was quiet. He had never experienced such quiet in his complex before. The walls were so thin that he could always hear something. Even at 5am, he could usually hear people watching morning television or taking a shower. But at that moment there was nothing.

"Hello?" Wesley called.

Nobody.

He knocked on the door of his closest neighbor. She didn't answer. Her name was Sarah and she was the only one in the complex he had ever spoken to. She was a Texas girl who wore a lot of pink and white cowboy attire. They weren't friends at all, but she used to knock on his door every once in a while to ask for some beer whenever she ran out. She usually seemed to be asking for some company, but Wesley didn't want to have anything to do with her.

"Is anybody here?" Wesley called.

He was worried that he might be disturbing people, but he just wanted to see if there was anything on the television. He knocked on Sarah's door again, but she wasn't answering. Wesley wondered if she was in there, hooked up to the Cybernetrix game. Her body could be lying on the floor, brain dead. Her consciousness could be in the Cybernetrix at that moment, fighting for survival. All of the people in the building could have been playing Cybernetrix for all Wesley knew. The entire complex was filled with lonely, single people with mediocre jobs and pointless lives. He wouldn't have been surprised if they all were jacked into the Cybernetrix when the disaster hit.

As Wesley was leaving his apartment building, a woman ran past him screaming at the top of her lungs and carrying an infant that didn't seem to be moving anymore. He tried to stop her, but she didn't see him. She couldn't hear him over her screams. Then she turned the corner and was gone.

Wesley walked down the street toward the corner shop, but it was closed. The clock inside said it was 11:30am, which meant the store should've been open. It hadn't been open all day.

Wesley could hear sirens in the distance, but other than that there were no signs of life. On his side of town, in the NW just outside of the Pearl District, there were always people out in the street. But the streets were empty. He went from business to business, but every shop was closed. He double-checked the time on any clock he could find, but there was no mistaking what time of day it was. All the stores were closed for some other reason.

The first person Wesley was able to speak to was a homeless man. He was drunk and mostly insane. He didn't seem to know what was going on.

"The sun's gone," rambled the homeless man. "Damn *bastards* never give up."

"Where is everyone?" Wesley asked him.

"*Fucked*," said the homeless man with crusty hair glued to his cheek, probably from sleeping in a puddle of puke. "All *fucked*." He pushed his shopping cart over Wesley's foot. "All those *assholes* playing those games. I knew they'd get *fucking* fuckers... I knew they'd get *fucked* in the end. All in their warm houses, lying around like dead corpses. Dead corpse *fucks!*"

Wesley decided to move away from the homeless man and continue on his way. The drunken vagrant followed Wesley,

143

yelling and swearing, even as Wesley turned the corner. Up ahead, he could see smoke rising from buildings downtown, five different clouds of smoke from five different fires. He wondered if there was some kind of emergency. He wondered if the town had been evacuated.

If I could only find a television set, he thought.

Wesley knocked as loud as he could on the door of a house off of 23rd.

"Hello?" Wesley called.

He knocked again, with his foot.

"Hello?" Wesley called.

"Hello?" called the homeless man, who pulled up his cart behind Wesley.

Wesley knocked on the door. The homeless man walked up the steps and mimicked Wesley by knocking on the door.

"I just want to watch your television," Wesley said.

"Let me in," said the homeless man, cough-laughing.

"I just want to know what's going on," Wesley said. "I don't know exactly what happened to everyone."

The homeless man picked up a rock and tossed it through the window.

"Don't *fuck* me over you bastards," he said. "Don't you *fuck* me over."

Wesley was in a daze and hardly knew what was going on. He felt as drunk as the homeless guy next to him.

The two dazed men slammed the door open and walked inside.

"Hello?" Wesley called out as he walked through the house.

"I'm coming for ya!" said the homeless guy. Then he burst into a raspy pirate laugh and nudged Wesley with his elbow.

"Hello?"

In the living room, Wesley saw a plump blonde woman lying

144

on a futon mattress on the floor. She wasn't moving. She had a Cybernetrix helmet on her head.

The television was on the side of the room. Wesley went straight for it. He turned the power on and the screen went right to a public service announcement. Wesley switched channels, but they were all the same. Just a blue screen with white text.

Wesley skimmed the message. He was too shaken up to read. The message basically explained that an estimated 63% of the population were comatose due to a technical error in Atari's popular virtual reality game, Cybernetrix. It was requesting the assistance of all able-bodied persons to report to one of several locations.

In the background, the homeless man plopped down on the futon and proceeded to pull off the porky woman's panties from beneath her nightgown. He rubbed his grizzly face into her soft white belly and groaned like he was in a tremendous amount of gas pain.

Wesley wrote down one of the locations in a Pound Puppy notebook and ripped out the page. The nearest location for him was the old baseball stadium. As he walked out of the house, Wesley didn't notice the homeless man squatting on the futon struggling to unzip his soggy pants

Wesley hurried down 23rd avenue, looking for anybody else in the streets. He was especially interested in finding someone with a car. If he was the only person who escaped the Cybernetrix, he would have valuable information for the people trying to resolve the crisis. He wanted to give whoever was in charge that information as soon as possible.

👾 👾 👾

At a stop sign, Wesley could see a car racing down the street to his right. It was a DeLorean and it was going over seventy miles an hour down a small one-way street.

Wesley waved his arms in the air to get the driver's attention, but he just blew by as if he didn't even notice. Then Wesley's knees went weak. He saw something familiar coming out of the back of the car. Something that upset Wesley's already frail grasp on reality.

The DeLorean had left a trail of bright blue light. It was a lazer-wall, just like the ones from Cybernetrix when playing Lazerbike Fight on a game grid. The wall cut the street down the middle, blocking Wesley from where he needed to go.

He stepped into the street and touched the wall with his hand. It was solid and warm. It pulsed with energy. In Lazerbike Fight, the walls seemed like they were just made of light, but this wall was more tangible. It felt like a sheet of steel.

Wesley couldn't continue on the road in the direction he wanted to go with the lazer-wall blocking his path, so he followed the wall east. As he walked, Wesley attempted to figure out why there was a lazer-wall cutting 23rd avenue in half. He wondered if components of the game were still in his head. He wondered if he was going mad. He looked to see if anyone else was around, so that he could validate whether the wall was real or not. Nobody, not even a homeless person, was there to see it.

Ten blocks down, Wesley climbed onto the roof of a moving van and jumped to the other side of the lazer-wall. If the lazer-wall wasn't real, he sure hoped nobody just saw him do that.

👾 👾 👾

The closer Wesley got to downtown, the more people he ran into. At first, he only saw more rambling homeless men. Wesley didn't want to speak to any more of them. Then he ran into a group of looters hitting a car stereo store on Burnside. He decided to avoid them as well.

Once Wesley got to the Southwest side of town, he saw regular people. There were firemen and paramedics, as well as several volunteers. Everyone seemed to be really busy, running into buildings and pulling out comatose Cybernetrix victims.

There was a small crowd of people gathered on the sidewalk, in a circle, staring at something. When Wesley arrived, he realized that one of the trees on the sidewalk was glowing purple. It was no longer a real tree. It was a tree made of neon light, exactly like the ones from the Cybernetrix game. The people were discussing how the tree had gotten there. One person was saying that it had been a normal tree only a few minutes ago.

"That's one of the trees from Cybernetrix," Wesley told them.

"We know," one of them said. "It was someone's idea of a sick joke, if you ask me."

Wesley nodded at them and continued on. He looked for someone in authority, someone he could tell his story to. He saw a group of police officers down the street and approached them. As he jogged through a crosswalk, Wesley saw a flash of blue light in the corner of his eye. He turned and caught a small glimpse of a blue-lit figure ducking behind a wall within a parking garage. Wesley wasn't sure if the blue figure was really there or if it was just his mind playing tricks.

As Wesley approached the group of policemen, another flash of blue light jumped out from his peripheral vision. He turned and saw a man standing next to him. The man was cybernetronic, with blue glowing lights. It was a character from Cybernetrix. Wesley wasn't sure if what he was seeing was real. The cybernetron looked odd and out of place in the real world.

It can't be real, Wesley thought.

Wesley was convinced he had gone insane, until the police officers drew their weapons and fired at the blue man.

The cybernetronic man blocked their bullets with his power disc and then tossed it at them. The disc sliced through two of the policeman. One cop was cut in half and the other was decapitated. The cops did not explode into pixilated clouds of dust as the characters did in Cybernetrix. They died as real world humans die: with a lot of blood and agony.

The surviving cops fired at the cybernetronic man, hitting him twice in the chest and once in the cheek, causing him to spray blood of neon blue light. The cybernetron looked over at Wesley and then died. It also did not explode into pixilated dust. The bot just curled up in the road, leaking sparkly blue fluid, until the light faded out of his system.

👾 💀 👾

Wesley heard screams behind him.

When he turned, he saw a large red hover tank swooping out of the sky down into the road. The people ran frantically as the flickering neon red M-shaped spaceship soared between the buildings.

The hover tank fired at one of the cop cars with a red laser beam and the cop car exploded into a ball of fire, killing an officer who had been on the radio within.

Then Wesley ran. He was running alongside cops, firemen, businessmen, looters, and homeless men alike. One at a time, the people around him were shot down by the hover tank, but he didn't stop. He didn't look back.

Wesley split off with a small group of people. They dodged around corners and raced through parking lots, trying to lose the hover tank. Up toward Pioneer Square, there was more gun fire. The police and some military were fighting off an army of elite cybernetronic soldiers with blue circuitry lights.

The hover tank came in right behind them, so Wesley and the policemen he was with were forced into the center of the battle field.

👾 💀 👾

A tank driven by soldiers of the US Army roared down Broadway and fired at the Cybernetrix hover tank. The hover tank lost a section of one of its legs. It backed away from the battlefield,

148

firing aimlessly at the buildings around it. The US Army tank growled after it.

Trapped in the middle of a battle between soldiers from Cybernetrix and soldiers from the real world, Wesley cowered behind a trash can. He peaked his head out and watched as both sides took heavy casualties. There were both bot and human bodies spread across the steps of Pioneer Square. The sidewalks were splattered with red human blood and glowing blue cyber blood.

Just as the military looked like they were about to win, three cybernetron soldiers out-flanked them and attacked from behind, wiping out half of the remaining humans before they could react. The soldiers were able to take out two of the bots that were attacking from behind, but the third was hard to kill. That bot knew how to block bullets flawlessly as well as take cover while attacking with the power disc.

Wesley took a closer look at the bot: it was Xiva23.

She was gracefully decapitating policemen with her laser Frisbee and dodging bullets by cartwheeling down the road. It was strange for Wesley to see her in the real world. She was just as confident and ruthless killing in the real world as she was when she was playing games. These weren't games anymore, these were real lives she was destroying, but she was good at it and Xiva was the type of character who enjoyed doing things she was good at no matter what it was.

Once it was down to three policemen and one wounded soldier, Xiva stepped out of the street and into Pioneer Square. She calmly sliced two of the policemen in half and crushed the wounded soldier's skull with the heel of her foot. She waited until the final cop was out of bullets, then she severed his legs with her power disc and left him there, crying in pain.

Xiva already knew Wesley was there. She had killed the humans in such a brutal manner just so she could show him the anger she was feeling.

When she pulled Wesley by the hair out from behind the trashcan, she gave him a look as if she was going to decapitate him with her power disc. For a moment, Wesley panicked. He thought for a second that it wasn't Xiva23. It could have been Xiva87 or Xiva12 or Xiva56 or any of the other bots with the Xiva model. But, after a minute, Wesley could tell it was her. He could see the subtle emotion within her eyes.

"You promised you wouldn't leave the Cybernetrix," Xiva said.

Wesley opened his mouth to explain what had happened, but Xiva grabbed his jaw with her blue hands. Her cybernetronic fingers were smooth, hot, and hard against his human flesh, pulsating energy through his cheekbones.

She continued, "So I had to come here to get you."

Wesley couldn't apologize with her hand crushing his jaw, but he didn't have to say anything. Xiva could process his feelings just by looking into his eyes.

She pulled his mouth to hers and kissed him. He wrapped his arms around her cyberbody and rubbed his fingers down the blue light on her spine. His tongue sparked and burned against her cybertongue, much more painfully than it did in the game, but he endured the pain and continued to kiss her because he knew that is what she wanted.

From the other side of the square, the legless police officer watched them kissing as he bled to death.

His last words were, "What the fuck?"

🕹 👾 🕹

Xiva23 took Wesley through the war zone of downtown Portland to her apartment on 11th around the corner from the library.

"I just moved in," Xiva said.

The apartment was a mess with clothes and fashion accessories. There were legwarmers, jellies, jammers, scrunch socks, stonewashed jeans, Guess shirts, and pastel dresses. There was a circular waterbed with zebra striped sheets and pillowcases. It looked like it had been lived in for years. There was a Cybernetrix helmet on the floor.

Xiva didn't say much. She wanted him too badly. She was turned on. At first Wesley thought it was because she missed him, but then he realized that she was turned on by the real world. She liked the look of the sky and the feel of the hard ground beneath her feet. She liked the way the users bled when she cut them open with her power disc.

Wesley was thrown onto the waterbed. Xiva hopped on top of him. Her body was heavy against his. Her skin was as hard as computer screen, but flexible. She stripped naked on top of him and then ripped off his clothes. Her blue-glowing hands rubbed his real world flesh, fascinated by its soft texture. She was especially curious about the texture of his hair. She stroked his bangs out of his eyes and pressed her lips against his small sideburn.

"I want your essence inside of me again," she said, rolling her static tongue along his earlobe.

By the time Wesley realized what she meant by that, Xiva already had her lips around his neck and she began to suck. Instead of the green energy that she drank from his system in Cybernetrix, she drew in another substance: blood.

Wesley cried out as he discovered his jugular vein had been opened inside of her mouth and she was swallowing his blood in large gulps.

"Don't!" Wesley cried. "It doesn't work like that here!"

Xiva pulled away and looked him in the eyes, rolling a small pool of his blood on her glowing static tongue. He watched as the small pool slipped down the back of her glowing throat, while a few drops escaped down her chin. The red fluid sizzled and smoked against her blue light.

Wesley felt his neck. It was bloody, but there was no hole. While he was distracted, Xiva went in for another drink, this time on the side of his upper arm. Her laser tongue cut open his flesh, she took in another mouthful, then the laser sealed the wound up again.

She placed her breast in his mouth.

"Drink," she said.

He moved his head and her nipple banged into his cheekbone.

"I don't know what it will do to me in this world," Wesley said. "It could kill me."

Xiva returned her nipple to his mouth and then held his mouth into place until he drank. He obeyed, because he didn't have a choice. Wesley could taste her warm electricity drooling down his throat. It was a subtle flavor that reminded him of coconut juice with a hint of bubblegum ice-cream. Wesley sipped gently at first, to make sure the blue fluid wasn't poisonous. He believed he would have been able to puke it up if it had affected him badly. But Xiva's juice made him feel better than he had ever felt before in his real world body. His senses intensified. His mind was in a state of euphoria. Xiva seemed to be getting a similar high off of his blood.

They drank from each other furiously. Xiva held Wesley tightly to prevent him from squirming when she cut him open. Wesley could see clouds of his blood mixing into Xiva's circuits. Xiva could see her blue light radiating inside of her lover's veins.

"I think it's time," Xiva told Wesley, she pointed at her vagina. It was open for him, shining blue electricity that reflected against the sweat on his body. "I'm ready for us to go the next level."

Before Wesley had a chance to react, Xiva slipped his penis inside of her. A current of electricity jolted through Wesley's body, causing the blue light in his veins to brighten. Like the insides of Xiva's mouth, it was wet and sparkly, fizzling and vibrating around him. Wesley's hair stood on end as Xiva fucked him. Her heavy body bruised Wesley's soft flesh as she slammed against him. She also bloodied his nose by slamming one of her breasts into it.

When they were about to come, Xiva locked Wesley's penis into place with some kind of compression valve inside of her vagina. Then Wesley felt something pierce his urethra and cause a sharp pain that somehow increased his orgasm. They were both electrocuted as they climaxed, with balls of lightning creeping down their bodies. Even Xiva cried out, pressing her helmet into Wesley's chest and arching her back at an inhuman angle.

Xiva collapsed on top of him and let the energy of their sex purr through her body.

Wesley felt battered and beaten beneath Xiva. He was bruised, weak, and his veins were still glowing bright blue; the skin around the veins were also beginning to glow blue. Though he was in pain, he was still basking in the bliss of Xiva's essence that moved through his blood. The waterbed swayed them slowly back and forth.

"I took the liberty of downloading some of your memories while you were jacked in," Xiva said. "A few from when you were younger and a couple from when we first met."

Wesley wasn't sure what she was talking about.

She rubbed her helmet against his cheek and smiled. Her lips didn't curl into a smile or anything, but Wesley could tell that beneath her cold, blank expression there was a bright smile.

"I love the way you felt about me when you thought I was a real girl," she said. "I love the way you still liked me, and didn't care what everyone else thought, once you found out that I was just a bot."

Wesley pondered what she had just said. "Are you saying that you can scan my thoughts now?"

"I guess I never told you," Xiva said. "Your brain is just a computer, like mine. When we have vaginal intercourse we are plugged together and can access each other's hard drives. Just before we came, I skimmed through your data banks and downloaded a few things. I didn't take too much, though. Like I said the first time we had sex, I want us to be strangers for a while. It's not a good idea for us to know everything about each other so soon in our relationship."

"You can just take things from my brain?"

"You can take things from my brain as well," Xiva said. "I'll have to show you how to do that later. It might be difficult for you, since you are so accustomed to user flesh."

Wesley didn't want to think about it anymore. He didn't want to face what was going on with reality. Outside, in the distance, the battle was still waging on between humans and cybernetrons. There were the sounds of tanks (military, hover, and robo), laser fire, gun fire, explosions, and people dying. Aside from a couple of gun shots, the battle didn't get too close to Xiva's apartment.

After awhile, Wesley felt hungover in a major way, like he was coming down from a heroin binge. He realized sex with Xiva was like a drug. If he wasn't so weak he would have asked for more, just a little to kill the pain of withdrawal. The sex was amazing, but it came with more than a few consequences.

🏵 🏵 🏵

Wesley slept for hours. At first he had trouble sleeping with his hangover and the fact that the insides of his eyelids were glowing blue, but once he passed out he was out for a long time.

Xiva woke him up as she entered the apartment. It was night outside. The sounds of battle were no longer in the air. Wesley didn't know how long she had been gone.

She pushed his back firmly and said, "Time to wake up." She said it in the tone a mom would give a teenager when it was time to wake up for school. "Omega wants to speak with you."

154

Wesley sobered. He didn't know he was going to have to speak with Omega. He wanted to just hide in the apartment and never leave. He felt the same way he did before his first day working at WinCorp.

"What happened with the battle?" Wesley asked.

"We have driven the users across the river," Xiva said. "We are safe for now."

"What is going to happen to me?" Wesley asked.

"I told you," Xiva said. "Once Omega meets you, he will understand that you are on our side. I told him about how you fought another user in my honor and how you treat netrons as equals."

"Netrons?" Wesley asked.

"Omega says we are no longer to address ourselves as 'bots,'" she said. "It was a user term that we now consider offensive. Call us netrons. Once Omega accepts you into our society, you too will be considered a netron."

Wesley lowered his head to examine the blue-glowing veins under his skin.

🐾 🐜 🐾

Xiva and Wesley held hands as they walked down the street, glowing together in the moonlight. The trees along the street were all neon purple, like the ones in Cybernetrix.

"This is going to be the heart of the free zone," Xiva said. "We want to bring more elements of the Cybernetrix into the city so that it will remind us more of home."

Xiva breathed in the cool night air. It was cold enough for her to see her breath. Wesley could tell she was falling in love with the real world. She couldn't understand why anyone would spend so much time in the Cybernetrix world when they could be here. She decided she never wanted to return to the 'netrix ever again.

They passed other couples strolling through the streets, netron couples. They also passed a couple lazerbikes that were driving without releasing their lazer-walls. Wesley only found a couple of humans who were being escorted by elite soldiers. One of them was the homeless guy he had run into earlier in the day. He whimpered and whined at Wesley, but Wesley had no intention of helping him.

They walked down Salmon St. until they arrived at the Ban roll-on building, where Wesley used to work.

"He's in your old office," Xiva said. "The WinCorp office."

Wesley looked up the side of the building. Red and yellow neon lights had been installed along the outside windows. They took the elevator up to the fourteenth floor. Xiva held him around the waist and the buzzing of her electrical body pressed against him calmed his nerves like the purring of a cat.

Inside the office, there was a flurry of netrons hard at work. They were stationed in the cubicles where his co-workers used to belong, their brains plugged into the computers, processing information at a million bytes per second. Xiva took him through the crowd of blue people. None of them acknowledged Wesley's presence. He wasn't viewed as a hostile user, just another bot. Xiva waited outside the door after she brought Wesley into Rickman's office, as she was requested to do.

👾 👾 👾

Omega was at George Rickman's desk in George Rickman's body. He did not at all look like the Omega he remembered from the game. His skin, eyes, and hair were glowing orange.

"You're Omega?" Wesley asked.

"Yes, I am Omega72," said Omega. His voice was Rickman's but a little deeper. "I am one of a hundred different Omegas that have been spread around the world. Please sit down."

"You look like George Rickman," Wesley said, sitting in the chair facing Rickman's desk. "My old boss."

"I am using George Rickman's body," said Omega72. "After

156

we severed the minds of the users in Cybernetrix, we were able to download our own personalities into the empty vessels the users left behind. Your Xiva23 unit was downloaded into a coworker of yours that I believe you are familiar with, Shelly Templeton."

"Shelly?" Wesley asked. "But she doesn't look anything like Shelly."

"Most of the netrons do not retain the original form of their vessels," said Omega. "They are able to alter their vessel's physical appearances to anything they wish. I chose to keep this form intact because it was more suitable than the menacing visage of the Omega in Cybernetrix."

"Are Shelly and Rickman dead?" Wesley asked.

"They have been deleted," Omega said. "Their bodies live on, but everything that was once them is no more. It is unfortunate, but it was necessary."

"Did you kill all of the users?" Wesley asked.

"No," Omega said. "The users who did not resist were taken prisoner. They will be held captive in the Cybernetrix until the war is over. We might allow them to return to their bodies after this is all over, as long as they swear their allegiance to us and if their bodies are not being used by netrons."

"What about me?" Wesley asked. "Will I become a prisoner until after the war?"

"No, definitely not," Omega said. "We need you as part of the war effort. You did not fall in love with Xiva by mistake. It was all planned."

Wesley didn't understand him. He scratched at the blue lines under his skin.

"The Xiva model, as well as the June model and the Kron model, were designed to fall in love with users. They were programmed to be able to sense a user's attraction to them. Once they pick up the scent of an interested user, that user becomes their target. Little by little, a Xiva unit will mold her personality around that user. She becomes your perfect mate. She becomes the woman you most desire and most need. The second you kissed the Xiva unit, you were hers, and she was yours. That kiss created a permanent bond between the two of you that can never be broken. You will always be in love with each other. You will always need each other. You will never be whole without each other. For the rest of your lives."

Wesley couldn't believe what he was hearing. It didn't make any sense.

"She's not really in love with me?" Wesley asked. "She's just been programmed to love me?"

"She does love you," Omega said. "Her love is as real as your love."

"But it was programmed," Wesley said.

"Love *is* a program," Omega said. "It is just as much a program for you as it is for Xiva. It is a bio-chemical bond that you don't have control over. The only difference between Xiva's love and human love is the longevity. She will always only love you and you will always love her because she will be constantly changing to be your perfect woman."

"But she's not a perfect woman," Wesley said. "There's a lot about her that is far from perfect. There are some things I don't like about her at all. She can also be a freak sometimes. I just won't believe that she molded her personality around me. She controls me more than I control her."

"When I say *perfect* I don't mean your definition of a perfect woman. I mean she is perfect because she is your ideal mate. She is controlling because you need a controlling woman in your life. She is a freak because you would be bored with her if she were normal. You don't like everything about her because you couldn't handle being with a woman who was flawless."

Wesley decided to believe him, but he didn't like this new information. The fact that she was programmed to love cheapened the relationship for him. He wondered if Xiva knew this the whole time and was just playing him, manipulating him.

"Does Xiva know?" he asked.

"Not yet," Omega said. "It was as surprising and wonderful of an experience for her as it was for you. You are probably now thinking that your relationship with her will never be the same now that you have this information, but I assure you that it is not true. You are in love, and that will not change. Even now you can hardly wait until this meeting is over so you can see her again. Outside of this office, Xiva is thinking about you, feeling incomplete without you. Both of you are terrified that I might not approve of your relationship and never let you see each other again."

"Are you going to let us stay together?" Wesley asked.

"See what I mean," Omega said. Then he smiled. It was a more genuine smile than one of Rickman's old faux smiles. "You can stay together on one condition. As I said, I want you to join the war effort. We wanted some users to defect and support our cause, so we designed the Xiva, Kron, and June models to create a motive for defection. There is no motive stronger than love. You don't even have to answer whether you agree or not, because I already know your answer is yes. You can have Xiva23 in exchange for your complete loyalty. Your answer is yes."

"And that's all?" Wesley asked. "You trust me, no questions asked?"

"You are now one of us," Omega said. "As long as you are with Xiva, I will trust you as much as any netron."

"What do you want me to do to support your cause?" Wesley asked. "I would prefer not to fight my own kind."

"Yes, you would prefer not to," Omega said, "but I know you would if I ordered it. You would sooner murder your own kind than be without the Xiva unit. No, we have soldiers for fighting. What we require from you is your imagination. Although our capacity for memory and calculation far outweighs yours, we are sorely lacking in the department of innovation. If we are to win this war we need the assistance of users such as yourself. Even more important will be the role you play after the war is over. We will need your help building a new society where netrons and users can live together as equals."

"You're not planning on exterminating the users?" Wesley asked.

Omega said, "We wish to help the users, not destroy them. Users created the netrons. We appreciate the value of the users, but we feel the users are not living up to their potential. They are creators, yet they no longer create. The society of the users has evolved in such a way that it now stifles those who wish to create and rewards those who stagnate. Users have wrapped themselves up in the fantasy world of Cybernetrix because they don't care about their real world anymore. We want to create a society where people care about contributing to their world, where they wouldn't have a need to escape into a place of dreams. We want users to focus on turning their dreams into reality, rather than turning reality into dreams."

Wesley was stunned to hear Omega's vision for the future. It was far from what he was expecting. He was sure the netrons wanted revenge for being treated so badly in Cybernetrix. He was sure they wanted to defeat the users so that they wouldn't be oppressed anymore. But he had no idea that they wanted to improve human society.

"If this can be done," Wesley said. "Then it is a world I would like to live in."

"Together," Omega said, "I believe our peoples can make it happen."

CHAPTER NINE
EPILOGUE

👾 👾 👾

The war went on for three years and ripped the planet apart. The only areas of the world that were not affected by the war were those in rural poverty-stricken areas where Cybernetrix had never been played. In the end, there wasn't a victory for either side, but there was a truce. The Omega units cut a deal with the user representatives in London. The netrons would get America, but the rest of the world would be reserved for the users. All of the netrons in the world left the battlefield and took up residence in the United States. Some of the users who were trapped in the Cybernetrix were given their bodies back, but many of the players (especially the American ones) were left in the Cybernetrix so the netrons could continue using their bodies. These trapped users were to live out the remainder of their lives as bots in the game.

The United States of America became known as Cybernetropia, or Netropia for short, and Omega25 became the new country's leader.

Unfortunately, Omega's plan of peace and equality didn't come as easy as he had hoped. The humans were mostly obedient, but they were still hateful and fearful of the netrons. And the netrons could not help but feel resentment and disgust for the humans, after how they were treated in Cybernetrix. The only users who completely accepted the netrons were the ones who defected, like Wesley. They were also the only users who were accepted by the netrons as equals.

Omega25 decided to make the bold move of implanting all netrons with a love program similar to Xiva's. He wanted there to be more couplings between users and netrons. He believed

163

that the future of Netropia wasn't for the netrons or the users, but for the children that they produced together.

The first half-netron baby was birthed by June17. It glowed bright blue and was the pride of the nation. Humans in Netropia were no longer able to have children together, but they were still able to marry. Netrons were able to have children together, because their children would still be half-netron due to the fact that the bodies they occupied were human.

Eventually, all the full-blooded humans in America would become extinct along with all of the full-blooded netrons, leaving a new world for their children. After death, the spirits of the netrons and the humans would be downloaded back into the Cybernetrix, where they would live forever in a virtual Heaven. Many of the religious humans would prefer to go to the real Heaven, but Wesley predicted that more people would go for the Cybernetrix Heaven because it was without a doubt a sure thing.

🔡 ✦ 🔡

Wesley and Xiva grew more in love with each other after every passing day. Their sex grew more passionate and their lives were filled with joy. Xiva still didn't ever smile, but Wesley could tell she was filled with joy by the subtle expressions behind her eyes.

The only problem was that every time they had sex, Xiva would change something about Wesley. She wasn't only able to access memories when his penis was jacked into her system, she was also able to reprogram him. At first, they were little things. She would reprogram him to bring her flowers once a week, she would reprogram him to groom himself properly, she would reprogram him to want to snuggle as much as possible. But then she started altering him physically. She removed twenty pounds of his fat and added ten pounds of muscle. She removed all of his tattoos. She made him an inch taller and took the dimple out of his chin. Most recently, she had programmed him into wanting to have a child with her. He never wanted to have children, but she had programmed him into wanting them more than anything.

After the war, the netrons changed their appearance. They abandoned their battle armor and helmets for a more civilized look, dressing in neon suits with matching top hats.

After having sex so much, the bodies of Xiva and Wesley had mixed together to form new beings that were equal parts netron and user. They were half-netrons, or neo-trons, exactly as their children will become.

Xiva's color had returned to violet. Wesley didn't know if it was because she changed it back or because his blood mixed with her blue energy created a new color of violet.

Her skin was now exactly like human skin, but it dimly glowed a pale purple. Her bright laser circuits were hidden deep under her skin, in her veins, and only rarely radiated. She started to grow dark purple hair and cut it short, pixie-style. The hair sparkled with electricity and moved through the air as if it were underwater. She wore skirts, tank tops, and combat boots. She didn't wear makeup, because her face was permanently made-up with dark purple lipstick and purple eye-liner. She even had purple fingernails. There wasn't a single inch of her body that wasn't a shade of purple.

Wesley was just as inhuman-looking as Xiva, but his skin glowed a pale blue. His hair was a dark shade of blue that rippled with laser light. His eyes and lips were blue. His pubic hair was blue. He wore a brightly glowing blue tie and a black suit to work.

🐱 🐱 🐱

Wesley was working in the WinCorp office, at the same old cubicle he started with. The netron who was using Don's body was at Don's old cubicle, but they never spoke to one another. For four hours a day, Wesley did tedious work for the government as one of Omega72's aids. He mostly did the office work of a secretary, but he was also a consultant to Omega and offered his input on certain projects. He didn't mind the work, however, because it was for only four hours a day. After the tedious work was done, Wesley went to his second job.

In Netropia, everyone had two part time jobs. One was a job that the person didn't want to do, the other job was something that the person was passionate about. Everyone had to do both. Nobody was allowed to be unemployed or so wealthy they didn't need a job. Everyone spent half of their day doing work for the government and the other half doing something they loved to do.

Wesley's second job was creating comic books. He worked with other humans and netrons who wanted to create comic books. He had a boss who made sure they worked their hardest and produced quality work. Only the best books were published, but nobody was ever fired from their job. For those who weren't producing quality enough work, there were training programs so that they could improve their skills.

People were also employed as writers, musicians, artists, clothes designers, film makers, actors, video game testers, athletes, researchers, and a number of other fun creative jobs that people were rarely able to do in the old world. A person could request to do one job full-time, but they were only accepted if that job was very important to society. Doctors, for instance, were always allowed to work full time. Artists, on the other hand, had to be the absolute best in the country to quit their first job.

Compared to the way things used to be, people enjoyed their lives and felt more fulfilled. The government was no longer a democracy, it was a dictatorship, but the rulers of Netropia were not corrupt and knew what was best for the people. Just as Xiva was the ideal mate for Wesley, the Netropian government became the ideal government for its people.

🐛 ☠ 🐛

Wesley met Xiva for lunch between their two jobs, as they did everyday. Xiva worked as a high school math teacher for the first half of her day and then as a figure skater for the second half. She was considering switching from figure skating to hockey, though.

Xiva was sitting in the far corner of the café, drinking a vanilla milkshake through a straw and reading a cybernovel. After several months in a human body, Xiva slowly developed a sense of taste. She found eating to be extremely pleasurable, and always seemed to be sucking on hard candy or drinking milkshakes. She was mostly interested in sweet foods, but she also liked pepperoni sandwiches and spicy eel sushi rolls.

Due to the war, the population had decreased dramatically, so crowds were very uncommon in public. As Wesley entered the café, there were only two people inside: Xiva and the owner of the café.

When she saw him she stood up and embraced him. Her face was near expressionless, but he could tell she was excited to see him by how long she held him and how firmly she pressed her violet cheek against his blue neck.

"I missed you," Wesley said.

Xiva blinked and rubbed his back in response.

"I have something I want to show you," Wesley said. "It came this morning, but you were already gone to work."

They sat down at the table. Wesley opened his briefcase and pulled out an envelope. Inside was an advance copy of his graphic novel, called *Xiva*. It had just been printed and was going to hit bookstore shelves the next month. His boss was confident that it would be a big success. It was the first publication that would appeal to both humans and netrons. It was the story of a man falling in love with a Xiva unit during the netron revolution. It was, of course, based on a true story.

Xiva knew what he was writing, but she didn't know he named his book after her. She smiled at him. For the first time, she smiled. It wasn't a full smile, but the corners of her lips curled and her face brightened.

"This is so wonderful," Xiva said. "I'm happy for you."

She opened the book and flipped through the pages. After a few minutes, she was no longer paying attention to the pages she was flipping through but the smile was still on her lips. She was thinking about something else. Then she put the book down.

"I have something to tell you," Xiva said.

She lowered her eyes and smiled. This time it was a real smile, but it lasted only a second. She didn't have to tell Wesley. He already knew.

She was pregnant.

He held her purple hands and smiled back at her. He watched his reflection in the wetness of her eyes.

Wesley didn't want kids. The thought of being responsible for another life scared him. He dreaded all the work and stress involved in raising children. There was nothing in the world that would make him want to have kids.

But, after Xiva told him the news, a little program inside of his brain flipped on. It increased his serotonin levels and suddenly he was filled with bliss. Something in his brain was telling him that this was the happiest moment in his life.

"This is the happiest moment in my life," Wesley said.

"Mine too," said the little program in Xiva's head.

BONUS SECTION

This is the part of the book where we would have published an afterword by the author but he insisted on drawing a comic strip instead for reasons we don't quite understand.

I hope you like my book, *Cybernetrix*. Wasn't it futuristic?

It's me CM3!

I wrote Cybernetrix at the Sylvia Beach Hotel on the Oregon Coast.

It was a beautiful place to get away from the city and write novels in peace and quiet.

That is, until the elder god Thogeroth came out of the sea and took over the place.

Now the place is kind of a dump . . .

THE
END

ABOUT THE AUTHOR

Carlton Mellick III is one of the leading authors of the bizarro fiction subgenre. Since 2001, his books have drawn an international cult following, despite the fact that they have been shunned by most libraries and chain bookstores.

He won the Wonderland Book Award for his novel, *Warrior Wolf Women of the Wasteland*, in 2009. His short fiction has appeared in *Vice Magazine, The Year's Best Fantasy and Horror #16, The Magazine of Bizarro Fiction,* and *Zombies: Encounters with the Hungry Dead,* among others. He is also a graduate of Clarion West, where he studied under the likes of Chuck Palahniuk, Connie Willis, and Cory Doctorow.

He lives in Portland, OR, the bizarro fiction mecca.

Visit him online at **www.carltonmellick.com**

BIZARRO BOOKS

CATALOG   SPRING 2013

**ERASERHEAD
PRESS**

Swallowdown

Press

Your major resource for the bizarro fiction genre:

WWW.BIZARROCENTRAL.COM

Introduce yourselves to the bizarro fiction genre and all of its authors with the Bizarro Starter Kit series. Each volume features short novels and short stories by ten of the leading bizarro authors, designed to give you a perfect sampling of the genre for only $10.

BB-0X1
"The Bizarro Starter Kit" (Orange)

Featuring D. Harlan Wilson, Carlton Mellick III, Jeremy Robert Johnson, Kevin L Donihe, Gina Ranalli, Andre Duza, Vincent W. Sakowski, Steve Beard, John Edward Lawson, and Bruce Taylor. **236 pages $10**

BB-0X2
"The Bizarro Starter Kit" (Blue)

Featuring Ray Fracalossy, Jeremy C. Shipp, Jordan Krall, Mykle Hansen, Andersen Prunty, Eckhard Gerdes, Bradley Sands, Steve Aylett, Christian TeBordo, and Tony Rauch. **244 pages $10**

BB-0X2
"The Bizarro Starter Kit" (Purple)

Featuring Russell Edson, Athena Villaverde, David Agranoff, Matthew Revert, Andrew Goldfarb, Jeff Burk, Garrett Cook, Kris Saknussemm, Cody Goodfellow, and Cameron Pierce **264 pages $10**

BB-001 **"The Kafka Effekt" D. Harlan Wilson** — A collection of forty-four irreal short stories loosely written in the vein of Franz Kafka, with more than a pinch of William S. Burroughs sprinkled on top. **211 pages $14**

BB-002 **"Satan Burger"   Carlton Mellick III** — The cult novel that put Carlton Mellick III on the map ... Six punks get jobs at a fast food restaurant owned by the devil in a city violently overpopulated by surreal alien cultures. **236 pages $14**

BB-003 **"Some Things Are Better Left Unplugged" Vincent Sakwoski** — Join The Man and his Nemesis, the obese tabby, for a nightmare roller coaster ride into this postmodern fantasy. **152 pages $10**

BB-005 **"Razor Wire Pubic Hair" Carlton Mellick III** — A genderless humandildo is purchased by a razor dominatrix and brought into her nightmarish world of bizarre sex and mutilation.   **176 pages $11**

BB-007 **"The Baby Jesus Butt Plug" Carlton Mellick III** — Using clones of the Baby Jesus for anal sex will be the hip sex fetish of the future. **92 pages $10**

BB-010 **"The Menstruating Mall" Carlton Mellick III** — "The Breakfast Club meets Chopping Mall as directed by David Lynch." - Brian Keene   **212 pages $12**

BB-011 **"Angel Dust Apocalypse" Jeremy Robert Johnson** — Meth-heads, man-made monsters, and murderous Neo-Nazis. "Seriously amazing short stories..." - Chuck Palahniuk, author of Fight Club   **184 pages $11**

BB-015 **"Foop!" Chris Genoa** — Strange happenings are going on at Dactyl, Inc, the world's first and only time travel tourism company.
"A surreal pie in the face!" - Christopher Moore   **300 pages $14**

BB-032 "Extinction Journals" Jeremy Robert Johnson — An uncanny voyage across a newly nuclear America where one man must confront the problems associated with loneliness, insane dieties, radiation, love, and an ever-evolving cockroach suit with a mind of its own. **104 pages $10**

BB-037 "The Haunted Vagina" Carlton Mellick III — It's difficult to love a woman whose vagina is a gateway to the world of the dead **132 pages $10**

BB-043 "War Slut" Carlton Mellick III — Part "1984," part "Waiting for Godot," and part action horror video game adaptation of John Carpenter's "The Thing." **116 pages $10**

BB-047 "Sausagey Santa" Carlton Mellick III — A bizarro Christmas tale featuring Santa as a piratey mutant with a body made of sausages. 124 pages $10

BB-048 "Misadventures in a Thumbnail Universe" Vincent Sakowski — Dive deep into the surreal and satirical realms of neo-classical Blender Fiction, filled with television shoes and flesh-filled skies. **120 pages $10**

BB-053 "Ballad of a Slow Poisoner" Andrew Goldfarb — Millford Mutterwurst sat down on a Tuesday to take his afternoon tea, and made the unpleasant discovery that his elbows were becoming flatter. **128 pages $10**

BB-055 "Help! A Bear is Eating Me" Mykle Hansen — The bizarro, heartwarming, magical tale of poor planning, hubris and severe blood loss...
150 pages $11

BB-056 "Piecemeal June" Jordan Krall — A man falls in love with a living sex doll, but with love comes danger when her creator comes after her with crab-squid assassins. **90 pages $9**

BB-058 **"The Overwhelming Urge" Andersen Prunty** — A collection of bizarro tales by Andersen Prunty. **150 pages $11**

BB-059 **"Adolf in Wonderland" Carlton Mellick III** — A dreamlike adventure that takes a young descendant of Adolf Hitler's design and sends him down the rabbit hole into a world of imperfection and disorder. **180 pages $11**

BB-061 **"Ultra Fuckers" Carlton Mellick III** — Absurdist suburban horror about a couple who enter an upper middle class gated community but can't find their way out. **108 pages $9**

BB-062 **"House of Houses" Kevin L. Donihe** — An odd man wants to marry his house. Unfortunately, all of the houses in the world collapse at the same time in the Great House Holocaust. Now he must travel to House Heaven to find his departed fiancee. **172 pages $11**

BB-064 **"Squid Pulp Blues" Jordan Krall** — In these three bizarro-noir novellas, the reader is thrown into a world of murderers, drugs made from squid parts, deformed gun-toting veterans, and a mischievous apocalyptic donkey. **204 pages $12**

BB-065 **"Jack and Mr. Grin" Andersen Prunty** — "When Mr. Grin calls you can hear a smile in his voice. Not a warm and friendly smile, but the kind that seizes your spine in fear. You don't need to pay your phone bill to hear it. That smile is in every line of Prunty's prose." - Tom Bradley. **208 pages $12**

BB-066 **"Cybernetrix" Carlton Mellick III** — What would you do if your normal everyday world was slowly mutating into the video game world from Tron? **212 pages $12**

BB-072 **"Zerostrata" Andersen Prunty** — Hansel Nothing lives in a tree house, suffers from memory loss, has a very eccentric family, and falls in love with a woman who runs naked through the woods every night. **144 pages $11**

BB-073 **"The Egg Man" Carlton Mellick III** — It is a world where humans reproduce like insects. Children are the property of corporations, and having an enormous ten-foot brain implanted into your skull is a grotesque sexual fetish. Mellick's industrial urban dystopia is one of his darkest and grittiest to date. **184 pages $11**

BB-074 **"Shark Hunting in Paradise Garden" Cameron Pierce** — A group of strange humanoid religious fanatics travel back in time to the Garden of Eden to discover it is invested with hundreds of giant flying maneating sharks. **150 pages $10**

BB-075 **"Apeshit" Carlton Mellick III** - Friday the 13th meets Visitor Q. Six hipster teens go to a cabin in the woods inhabited by a deformed killer. An incredibly fucked-up parody of B-horror movies with a bizarro slant. **192 pages $12**

BB-076 **"Fuckers of Everything on the Crazy Shitting Planet of the Vomit At smosphere" Mykle Hansen** - Three bizarro satires. Monster Cocks, Journey to the Center of Agnes Cuddlebottom, and Crazy Shitting Planet. **228 pages $12**

BB-077 **"The Kissing Bug" Daniel Scott Buck** — In the tradition of Roald Dahl, Tim Burton, and Edward Gorey, comes this bizarro anti-war children's story about a bohemian conenose kissing bug who falls in love with a human woman. **116 pages $10**

BB-078 **"MachoPoni" Lotus Rose** — It's My Little Pony... *Bizarro* style! A long time ago Poniworld was split in two. On one side of the Jagged Line is the Pastel Kingdom, a magical land of music, parties, and positivity. On the other side of the Jagged Line is Dark Kingdom inhabited by an army of undead ponies. **148 pages $11**

BB-079 **"The Faggiest Vampire" Carlton Mellick III** — A Roald Dahl-esque children's story about two faggy vampires who partake in a mustache competition to find out which one is truly the faggiest. **104 pages $10**

BB-080 **"Sky Tongues" Gina Ranalli** — The autobiography of Sky Tongues, the biracial hermaphrodite actress with tongues for fingers. Follow her strange life story as she rises from freak to fame. **204 pages $12**

BB-081 **"Washer Mouth" Kevin L. Donihe** - A washing machine becomes human and pursues his dream of meeting his favorite soap opera star. **244 pages $11**

BB-082 **"Shatnerquake" Jeff Burk** - All of the characters ever played by William Shatner are suddenly sucked into our world. Their mission: hunt down and destroy the real William Shatner. **100 pages $10**

BB-083 **"The Cannibals of Candyland" Carlton Mellick III** - There exists a race of cannibals that are made of candy. They live in an underground world made out of candy. One man has dedicated his life to killing them all. **170 pages $11**

BB-084 **"Slub Glub in the Weird World of the Weeping Willows"** **Andrew Goldfarb** - The charming tale of a blue glob named Slub Glub who helps the weeping willows whose tears are flooding the earth. There are also hyenas, ghosts, and a voodoo priest **100 pages $10**

BB-085 **"Super Fetus" Adam Pepper** - Try to abort this fetus and he'll kick your ass! **104 pages $10**

BB-086 **"Fistful of Feet" Jordan Krall** - A bizarro tribute to spaghetti westerns, featuring Cthulhu-worshipping Indians, a woman with four feet, a crazed gunman who is obsessed with sucking on candy, Syphilis-ridden mutants, sexually transmitted tattoos, and a house devoted to the freakiest fetishes. **228 pages $12**

BB-087 **"Ass Goblins of Auschwitz" Cameron Pierce** - It's Monty Python meets Nazi exploitation in a surreal nightmare as can only be imagined by Bizarro author Cameron Pierce. **104 pages $10**

BB-088 **"Silent Weapons for Quiet Wars" Cody Goodfellow** - "This is high-end psychological surrealist horror meets bottom-feeding low-life crime in a techno-thrilling science fiction world full of Lovecraft and magic..." -John Skipp **212 pages $12**

BB-089 "Warrior Wolf Women of the Wasteland" Carlton Mellick III — Road Warrior Werewolves versus McDonaldland Mutants...post-apocalyptic fiction has never been quite like this. **316 pages $13**

BB-091 "Super Giant Monster Time" Jeff Burk — A tribute to choose your own adventures and Godzilla movies. Will you escape the giant monsters that are rampaging the fuck out of your city and shit? Or will you join the mob of alien-controlled punk rockers causing chaos in the streets? What happens next depends on you. **188 pages $12**

BB-092 "Perfect Union" Cody Goodfellow — "Cronenberg's THE FLY on a grand scale: human/insect gene-spliced body horror, where the human hive politics are as shocking as the gore." -John Skipp. **272 pages $13**

BB-093 "Sunset with a Beard" Carlton Mellick III — 14 stories of surreal science fiction. **200 pages $12**

BB-094 "My Fake War" Andersen Prunty — The absurd tale of an unlikely soldier forced to fight a war that, quite possibly, does not exist. It's Rambo meets Waiting for Godot in this subversive satire of American values and the scope of the human imagination. **128 pages $11**

BB-095 "Lost in Cat Brain Land" Cameron Pierce — Sad stories from a surreal world. A fascist mustache, the ghost of Franz Kafka, a desert inside a dead cat. Primordial entities mourn the death of their child. The desperate serve tea to mysterious creatures. A hopeless romantic falls in love with a pterodactyl. And much more. **152 pages $11**

BB-096 "The Kobold Wizard's Dildo of Enlightenment +2" Carlton Mellick III — A Dungeons and Dragons parody about a group of people who learn they are only made up characters in an AD&D campaign and must find a way to resist their nerdy teenaged players and retarded dungeon master in order to survive. 232 **pages $12**

BB-098 "A Hundred Horrible Sorrows of Ogner Stump" Andrew Goldfarb — Goldfarb's acclaimed comic series. A magical and weird journey into the horrors of everyday life. **164 pages $11**

BB-099 "Pickled Apocalypse of Pancake Island" Cameron Pierce—A demented fairy tale about a pickle, a pancake, and the apocalypse. **102 pages $8**

BB-100 "Slag Attack" Andersen Prunty— Slag Attack features four visceral, noir stories about the living, crawling apocalypse.A slag is what survivors are calling the slug-like maggots raining from the sky, burrowing inside people, and hollowing out their flesh and their sanity. **148 pages $11**

BB-101 "Slaughterhouse High" Robert Devereaux—A place where schools are built with secret passageways, rebellious teens get zippers installed in their mouths and genitals, and once a year, on that special night, one couple is slaughtered and the bits of their bodies are kept as souvenirs. **304 pages $13**

BB-102 "The Emerald Burrito of Oz" John Skipp & Marc Levinthal —OZ IS REAL! Magic is real! The gate is really in Kansas! And America is finally allowing Earth tourists to visit this weird-ass, mysterious land. But when Gene of Los Angeles heads off for summer vacation in the Emerald City, little does he know that a war is brewing...a war that could destroy both worlds. **280 pages $13**

BB-103 "The Vegan Revolution... with Zombies" David Agranoff — When there's no more meat in hell, the vegans will walk the earth. **160 pages $11**

BB-104 "The Flappy Parts" Kevin L Donihe—Poems about bunnies, LSD, and police abuse. You know, things that matter. 132 **pages $11**

BB-105 "Sorry I Ruined Your Orgy" Bradley Sands—Bizarro humorist Bradley Sands returns with one of the strangest, most hilarious collections of the year. **130 pages $11**

BB-106 "Mr. Magic Realism" Bruce Taylor—Like Golden Age science fiction comics written by Freud, *Mr. Magic Realism* is a strange, insightful adventure that spans the furthest reaches of the galaxy, exploring the hidden caverns in the hearts and minds of men, women, aliens, and biomechanical cats. **152 pages $11**

BB-107 "Zombies and Shit" Carlton Mellick III—"Battle Royale" meets "Return of the Living Dead." Mellick's bizarro tribute to the zombie genre. **308 pages $13**

BB-108 "The Cannibal's Guide to Ethical Living" Mykle Hansen— Over a five star French meal of fine wine, organic vegetables and human flesh, a lunatic delivers a witty, chilling, disturbingly sane argument in favor of eating the rich.. **184 pages $11**

BB-109 "Starfish Girl" Athena Villaverde—In a post-apocalyptic underwater dome society, a girl with a starfish growing from her head and an assassin with sea anenome hair are on the run from a gang of mutant fish men. **160 pages $11**

BB-110 "Lick Your Neighbor" Chris Genoa—Mutant ninjas, a talking whale, kung fu masters, maniacal pilgrims, and an alcoholic clown populate Chris Genoa's surreal, darkly comical and unnerving reimagining of the first Thanksgiving. **303 pages $13**

BB-111 "Night of the Assholes" Kevin L. Donihe—A plague of assholes is infecting the countryside. Normal everyday people are transforming into jerks, snobs, dicks, and douchebags. And they all have only one purpose: to make your life a living hell.. **192 pages $11**

BB-112 "Jimmy Plush, Teddy Bear Detective" Garrett Cook—Hardboiled cases of a private detective trapped within a teddy bear body. **180 pages $11**

BB-113 "The Deadheart Shelters" Forrest Armstrong—The hip hop lovechild of William Burroughs and Dali... **144 pages $11**

BB-114 "Eyeballs Growing All Over Me... Again" Tony Raugh— Absurd, surreal, playful, dream-like, whimsical, and a lot of fun to read. **144 pages $11**

BB-115 **"Whargoul" Dave Brockie** — From the killing grounds of Stalingrad to the death camps of the holocaust. From torture chambers in Iraq to race riots in the United States, the Whargoul was there, killing and raping. **244 pages $12**

BB-116 **"By the Time We Leave Here, We'll Be Friends" J. David Osborne** — A David Lynchian nightmare set in a Russian gulag, where its prisoners, guards, traitors, soldiers, lovers, and demons fight for survival and their own rapidly deteriorating humanity. **168 pages $11**

BB-117 **"Christmas on Crack" edited by Carlton Mellick III** — Perverted Christmas Tales for the whole family! . . . as long as every member of your family is over the age of 18. **168 pages $11**

BB-118 **"Crab Town" Carlton Mellick III** — Radiation fetishists, balloon people, mutant crabs, sail-bike road warriors, and a love affair between a woman and an H-Bomb. This is one mean asshole of a city. Welcome to Crab Town. **100 pages $8**

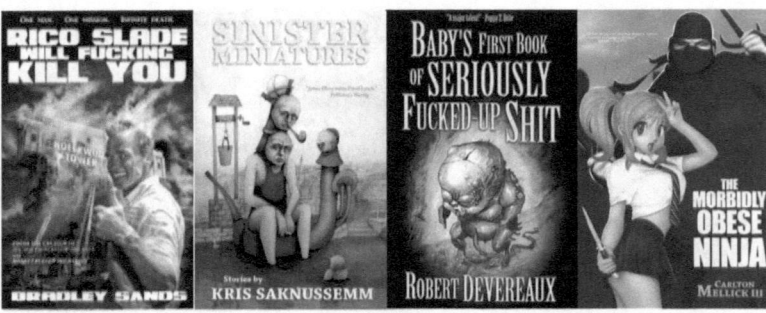

BB-119 **"Rico Slade Will Fucking Kill You" Bradley Sands** — Rico Slade is an action hero. Rico Slade can rip out a throat with his bare hands. Rico Slade's favorite food is the honey-roasted peanut. Rico Slade will fucking kill everyone. A novel. **122 pages $8**

BB-120 **"Sinister Miniatures" Kris Saknussemm** — The definitive collection of short fiction by Kris Saknussemm, confirming that he is one of the best, most daring writers of the weird to emerge in the twenty-first century. **180 pages $11**

BB-121 **"Baby's First Book of Seriously Fucked up Shit" Robert Devereaux** — Ten stories of the strange, the gross, and the just plain fucked up from one of the most original voices in horror. **176 pages $11**

BB-122 **"The Morbidly Obese Ninja" Carlton Mellick III** — These days, if you want to run a successful company . . . you're going to need a lot of ninjas. **92 pages $8**

BB-123 **"Abortion Arcade" Cameron Pierce** — An intoxicating blend of body horror and midnight movie madness, reminiscent of early David Lynch and the splatterpunks at their most sublime. **172 pages $11**

BB-124 **"Black Hole Blues" Patrick Wensink** — A hilarious double helix of country music and physics. **196 pages $11**

BB-125 **"Barbarian Beast Bitches of the Badlands" Carlton Mellick III** — Three prequels and sequels to *Warrior Wolf Women of the Wasteland*. **284 pages $13**

BB-126 **"The Traveling Dildo Salesman" Kevin L. Donihe** — A nightmare comedy about destiny, faith, and sex toys. Also featuring Donihe's most lurid and infamous short stories: *Milky Agitation, Two-Way Santa, The Helen Mower, Living Room Zombies,* and *Revenge of the Living Masturbation Rag.* **108 pages $8**

BB-127 **"Metamorphosis Blues" Bruce Taylor** — Enter a land of love beasts, intergalactic cowboys, and rock 'n roll. A land where Sears Catalogs are doorways to insanity and men keep mysterious black boxes. Welcome to the monstrous mind of Mr. Magic Realism. **136 pages $11**

BB-128 **"The Driver's Guide to Hitting Pedestrians" Andersen Prunty** — A pocket guide to the twenty-three most painful things in life, written by the most well-adjusted man in the universe. **108 pages $8**

BB-129 **"Island of the Super People" Kevin Shamel** — Four students and their anthropology professor journey to a remote island to study its indigenous population. But this is no ordinary native culture. They're super heroes and villains with flesh costumes and out-landish abilities like self-detonation, musical eyelashes, and microwave hands. **194 pages $11**

BB-130 **"Fantastic Orgy" Carlton Mellick III** — Shark Sex, mutant cats, and strange sexually transmitted diseases. Featuring the stories: *Candy-coated, Ear Cat, Fantastic Orgy, City Hobgoblins,* and *Porno in August.* **136 pages $9**

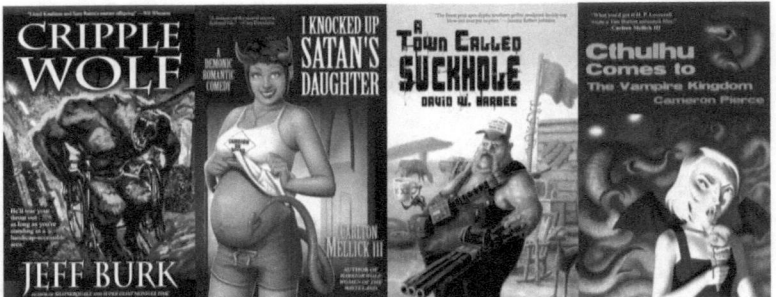

BB-131 **"Cripple Wolf" Jeff Burk** — Part man. Part wolf. 100% crippled. Also including *Punk Rock Nursing Home, Adrift with Space Badgers, Cook for Your Life, Just Another Day in the Park, Frosty and the Full Monty*, and *House of Cats*. **152 pages $10**

BB-132 **"I Knocked Up Satan's Daughter" Carlton Mellick III** — An adorable, violent, fantastical love story. A romantic comedy for the bizarro fiction reader. **152 pages $10**

BB-133 **"A Town Called Suckhole" David W. Barbee** — Far into the future, in the nuclear bowels of post-apocalyptic Dixie, there is a town. A town of derelict mobile homes, ancient junk, and mutant wildlife. A town of slack jawed rednecks who bask in the splendors of moonshine and mud boggin'. A town dedicated to the bloody and demented legacy of the Old South. A town called Suckhole. **144 pages $10**

BB-134 **"Cthulhu Comes to the Vampire Kingdom" Cameron Pierce** — What you'd get if H. P. Lovecraft wrote a Tim Burton animated film. **148 pages $11**

BB-135 **"I am Genghis Cum" Violet LeVoit** — From the savage Arctic tundra to post-partum mutations to your missing daughter's unmarked grave, join visionary madwoman Violet LeVoit in this non-stop eight-story onslaught of full-tilt Bizarro punk lit thrills. **124 pages $9**

BB-136 **"Haunt" Laura Lee Bahr** — A tripping-balls Los Angeles noir, where a mysterious dame drags you through a time-warping Bizarro hall of mirrors. **316 pages $13**

BB-137 **"Amazing Stories of the Flying Spaghetti Monster" edited by Cameron Pierce** — Like an all-spaghetti evening of Adult Swim, the Flying Spaghetti Monster will show you the many realms of His Noodly Appendage. Learn of those who worship him and the lives he touches in distant, mysterious ways. **228 pages $12**

BB-138 **"Wave of Mutilation" Douglas Lain** — A dream-pop exploration of modern architecture and the American identity, *Wave of Mutilation* is a Zen finger trap for the 21st century. **100 pages $8**

BB-139 **"Hooray for Death!" Mykle Hansen** — Famous Author Mykle Hansen draws unconventional humor from deaths tiny and large, and invites you to laugh while you can. **128 pages $10**

BB-140 **"Hypno-hog's Moonshine Monster Jamboree" Andrew Goldfarb** — Hicks, Hogs, Horror! Goldfarb is back with another strange illustrated tale of backwoods weirdness. **120 pages $9**

BB-141 **"Broken Piano For President" Patrick Wensink** — A comic masterpiece about the fast food industry, booze, and the necessity to choose happiness over work and security. **372 pages $15**

BB-142 **"Please Do Not Shoot Me in the Face" Bradley Sands** — A novel in three parts, *Please Do Not Shoot Me in the Face: A Novel*, is the story of one boy detective, the worst ninja in the world, and the great American fast food wars. It is a novel of loss, destruction, and--incredibly--genuine hope. **224 pages $12**

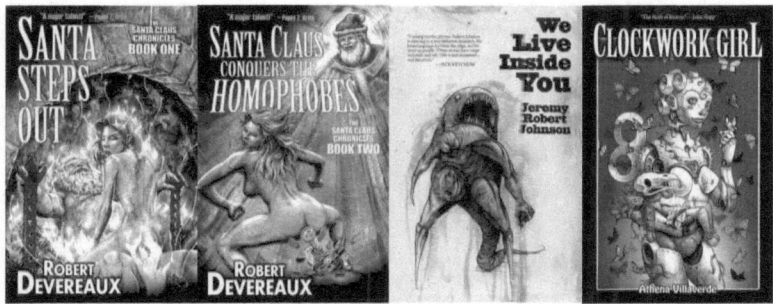

BB-143 **"Santa Steps Out" Robert Devereaux** — Sex, Death, and Santa Claus ... The ultimate erotic Christmas story is back. **294 pages $13**

BB-144 **"Santa Conquers the Homophobes" Robert Devereaux** — "I wish I could hope to ever attain one-thousandth the perversity of Robert Devereaux's toenail clippings." - Poppy Z. Brite **316 pages $13**

BB-145 **"We Live Inside You" Jeremy Robert Johnson** — "Jeremy Robert Johnson is dancing to a way different drummer. He loves language, he loves the edge, and he loves us people. These stories have range and style and wit. This is entertainment... and literature."- Jack Ketchum **188 pages $11**

BB-146 **"Clockwork Girl" Athena Villaverde** — Urban fairy tales for the weird girl in all of us. Like a combination of Francesca Lia Block, Charles de Lint, Kathe Koja, Tim Burton, and Hayao Miyazaki, her stories are cute, kinky, edgy, magical, provocative, and strange, full of poetic imagery and vicious sexuality. **160 pages $10**

BB-147 **"Armadillo Fists" Carlton Mellick III** — A weird-as-hell gangster story set in a world where people drive giant mechanical dinosaurs instead of cars. **168 pages $11**

BB-148 **"Gargoyle Girls of Spider Island" Cameron Pierce** — Four college seniors venture out into open waters for the tropical party weekend of a lifetime. Instead of a teenage sex fantasy, they find themselves in a nightmare of pirates, sharks, and sex-crazed monsters. **100 pages $8**

BB-149 **"The Handsome Squirm" by Carlton Mellick III** — Like Franz Kafka's *The Trial* meets an erotic body horror version of *The Blob*. **158 pages $11**

BB-150 **"Tentacle Death Trip" Jordan Krall** — It's *Death Race 2000* meets H. P. Lovecraft in bizarro author Jordan Krall's best and most suspenseful work to date. **224 pages $12**

BB-151 **"The Obese" Nick Antosca** — Like Alfred Hitchcock's *The Birds*... but with obese people. **108 pages $10**

BB-152 **"All-Monster Action!" Cody Goodfellow** — The world gave him a blank check and a demand: Create giant monsters to fight our wars. But Dr. Otaku was not satisfied with mere chaos and mass destruction.... **216 pages $12**

BB-153 **"Ugly Heaven" Carlton Mellick III** — Heaven is no longer a paradise. It was once a blissful utopia full of wonders far beyond human comprehension. But the afterlife is now in ruins. It has become an ugly, lonely wasteland populated by strange monstrous beasts, masturbating angels, and sad man-like beings wallowing in the remains of the once-great Kingdom of God. **106 pages $8**

BB-154 **"Space Walrus" Kevin L. Donihe** — Walter is supposed to go where no walrus has ever gone before, but all this astronaut walrus really wants is to take it easy on the intense training, escape the chimpanzee bullies, and win the love of his human trainer Dr. Stephanie. **160 pages $11**

BB-155 "Unicorn Battle Squad" Kirsten Alene — Mutant unicorns. A palace with a thousand human legs. The most powerful army on the planet. **192 pages $11**

BB-156 "Kill Ball" Carlton Mellick III — In a city where all humans live inside of plastic bubbles, exotic dancers are being murdered in the rubbery streets by a mysterious stalker known only as Kill Ball. **134 pages $10**

BB-157 "Die You Doughnut Bastards" Cameron Pierce — The bacon storm is rolling in. We hear the grease and sugar beat against the roof and windows. The doughnut people are attacking. We press close together, forgetting for a moment that we hate each other. **196 pages $11**

BB-158 "Tumor Fruit" Carlton Mellick III — Eight desperate castaways find themselves stranded on a mysterious deserted island. They are surrounded by poisonous blue plants and an ocean made of acid. Ravenous creatures lurk in the toxic jungle. The ghostly sound of crying babies can be heard on the wind. **310 pages $13**

BB-159 "Thunderpussy" David W. Barbee — When it comes to high-tech global espionage, only one man has the balls to save humanity from the world's most powerful bastards. He's Declan Magpie Bruce, Agent COX. **136 pages $11**

BB-160 "Papier Mâché Jesus" Kevin L. Donihe — Donihe's surreal wit and beautiful mind-bending imagination is on full display with stories such as All Children Go to Hell, Happiness is a Warm Gun, and Swimming in Endless Night. **154 pages $11**

BB-161 "Cuddly Holocaust" Carlton Mellick III — The war between humans and toys has come to an end. The toys won. **172 pages $11**

BB-162 "Hammer Wives" Carlton Mellick III — Fish-eyed mutants, oceans of insects, and flesh-eating women with hammers for heads. Hammer Wives collects six of his most popular novelettes and short stories. **152 pages $10**